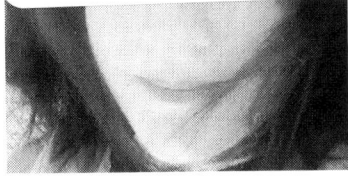

My name is J L Thomas and as a young child, I was an avid lover of the written word. Now that I am all grown up, I still find words truly intriguing and wholly inspiring. I spend most of my days in my precious writing cave and along with my muse (who, I must add, is relentless in her task to get me to stop surfing Pinterest for more photographic inspiration!) we create romantic/erotic stories and along the way, we *breathe* precious life into what we feel are some rather enchanting characters... Ones that we hope will capture the reader's imagination, transport them into the beating-heart of the story and remain buried deep within their souls forever.

The Gentle Dominant

J L Thomas

The Gentle Dominant

Chimera

CHIMERA PAPERBACK

© Copyright 2016
J L Thomas

The right of J L Thomas to be identified as author of
this work has been asserted by her in accordance with the
Copyright, Designs and Patents Act 1988.

All Rights Reserved

No reproduction, copy or transmission of this publication
may be made without written permission.
No paragraph of this publication may be reproduced,
copied or transmitted save with the written permission or in accordance
with the provisions
of the Copyright Act 1956 (as amended).

Any person who commits any unauthorised act in relation to
this publication may be liable to criminal
prosecution and civil claims for damages.

A CIP catalogue record for this title is
available from the British Library.

ISBN 978 1903136 51 5

This is a work of fiction. Names, characters, businesses, places, events and
incidents are either the products of the author's imagination or used in a
fictitious manner. Any resemblance to actual persons, living or dead, or
actual events is purely coincidental.

Chimera is an imprint of
Pegasus Elliot MacKenzie Publishers Ltd.
www.pegasuspublishers.com

First Published in 2016

Chimera
Sheraton House Castle Park
Cambridge England

Printed & Bound in Great Britain

Dedicated to everyone who thinks I am writing about them.

I am.

Contents

The Unravelling Of Theo	11
The Gentle Dominant	67
"Forever Yours"	109

THE UNRAVELLING OF THEO

True love never dies, it only sleeps for a little while…

My heart is aflame as he lifts me into his strong arms. We've been afar from each other for too long now. Our time to join souls has finally arrived. Without a single word passing between us, we close our eyes. The mist of time silently envelopes us in her waiting arms, and while the fragments of our memories that have lain dormant for centuries past slowly begin to resurface, and in the calmness of her wake, we become as one.

CHAPTER ONE

Gingerly poking my Greek salad around the plate, my thoughts wandered back to the horrific scene this afternoon in my boss's office and his spiteful grounding words that echoed around the room as I fled out of the foyer of my workplace – words that were not only untrue but painfully detrimental towards my character: "You're fired, Eden. You've been here less than six months and in that time, you have created nothing but *chaos*!"

What he meant to say… what he should've been honest and admitted was: 'Because I wouldn't give into his sexual desires, I was now redundant to his requirements.'

I was almost ready to prepare for going home, when he had called me into his office and beckoned me to come around to his side of the desk. Not thinking anything unusual of his request, as this was the normal run of the mill for him to ask, I obliged. Standing next to him, he tapped the buff-coloured dossier that was resting on top of the table and told me to read the contents, which contained my latest edits on his choice of a romance novel – one which I knew he was hoping would make the top ten reading list of 2015, I leant over to open the cover and that was when he sidled up so close to me that I could smell his foul cigarette-stenched breath, and as it settled upon my neck, I had to try extremely hard to stifle a gag that was building in the back of my throat.

He was now too close for comfort and I was beginning to feel intimidated. Sliding his hand along the curve of my buttock, he lightly slapped my behind and informed me that the next time I showed him my rather shoddy edits, I would most definitely be on the receiving end of one of his much harder spanks. I was now rigid with fear. I tried to move away but he slid his hand up under the back of my skirt and began to run his hand up my inner thigh. Now feeling utterly enraged, I found my courage, swung around and slapped him full-force on the cheek. Watching him reel back from the shock of the impact, the adrenaline now pouring into my bloodstream, I started shaking. Backing away from him, I turned and scooted towards the door only to stop dead in my tracks when I heard his voice boom, "Don't you dare walk out on me, Eden! You had better stop and apologise for striking me or you won't be working here any more."

His words now maddening me, I turned, and when I saw the evil, calculating look in his eyes, I knew I would have to win this battle. There was no way I was going let him humiliate me sexually or browbeat me verbally. He started to laugh and began to approach me. On reaching me, he roughly grasped me by the wrist and yanked my arm so hard that I let out a yelp.

"Stop making a fuss, sweetheart," he rasped. "I know ever since your started working here, you've been gagging for me to fuck you."

I didn't say another word. To ease myself out of this frightening situation, I just let him think I was game, so I let my body go slightly limp and assisted him in letting him drag me towards the couch. He pushed me backwards. I fell flush to the cushions and found myself splayed out like a waiting target. Shrugging out of his jacket, he loosened his tie and I stilled as his large hands travelled towards the top of his trousers. Still cackling at me, he began to undo his belt. Hearing the *whoosh* of it as it pulled it from the loops and the snap as he slapped it against his palm caused me to shudder.

"Oh you little teasing bitch," he smirked. "You've done nothing but tempt me for months with your short skirts and high heels. And now, when I finally give in to your wonton charms, you slap me for my generosity. So for that display of rather naughty behaviour, I am going to enjoy teaching you a lesson."

The second he called me 'a teasing little bitch', something snapped within me. All fear left me and I felt braver than ever. I scurried to my feet, stood tall, and squaring up right in front of him, I offered, "So, you want to punish me with your belt, do you? With each welt of your leather sending my buttocks red raw, you think you will be getting me so wet that you can ram your manhood into me with ease? Do you? Does the thought of fucking me senseless from behind while I scream out your name and beg with you to pound into me harder turn you on? Does it?"

We were eye-to-eye and the stark look of surprise that had spread across his face was priceless. It was an amusing combination of shock, which was splattered with a soupçon of triumph, and I for one was going to enjoy wiping that ridiculous smug look that was plastered on his face and propelling it head-first into the next dimension. He leant in towards me; I hitched a breath and encouraged him to clasp his fingers around my throat. I told him that was exactly how I like to be treated before I'm taken. He menacingly leant into me, hovered his lips above mine and growled, "So, you do want me after all? I knew you were the type of woman who likes a hard spanking with a good, hard fuck to follow!"

"Of course I am and of course I do," I laughed. "How could any woman possibly resist a red-blooded man like you? I've been waiting for this moment for so long but first I want to see what it feels like to kiss you. I want to feel the warmth, the wetness of your tongue as it hungrily scrolls around mine."

He didn't say another word. He just tightened his grip around my neck and crushed his lips to mine.

He shouldn't have done that! My knee came up full force and as I slammed it into his groin, the sound he made was a cross between a whimper and a deep extension of an ongoing moan. Watching him as he crumpled to his knees and rolled onto his side, I took immense pleasure in stooping down, picking up his belt and stepping over him. While he squirmed and spluttered for his breath, I took a few steps towards the door, turned and threw his belt at him at him while sarcastically asking, "Do your balls ache and does your cock feel humiliated? How's your ego now? Is it lost somewhere between your trembling thighs?"

That was the moment when I saw the brooding, almost darkened glare in his teared-up eyes, and I decided enough was enough – and even though I was as scared as could be, I regained my composure, and as confidently as I could, I strutted out of the room.

Hence, this is the real reason why he fired me: for *not* putting up with sexual harassment in the workplace.

CHAPTER TWO

Staring at a lone cube of feta cheese, I stab it with my fork and inwardly chuckle to myself while I imagine it to be my ex-boss' hopefully still aching groin! Lost in my own little creative world, I swirl said cheese into the creamy dressing and as I go to prod it again, a rather smooth and sultry voice whispers in my ear, "It's not that bad, you know. Try popping it in that pretty little mouth of yours and devouring its tart flavour. I can assure you, you will like it."

I groan. I'm really not in the mood for another feisty duel with another ego-fuelled man. I glance upwards with the full intent of asking this person to go away, but as I catch the owner of the voices' gaze, and as I see him for the every first time, I can't move a muscle. I'm now rigid – but not with fear. Instead, I am glued to my seat by this man's infectious, almost god-like presence. To say he is absolutely drop-dead gorgeous would be an understatement. He is positively angelic. His thick, curly, blond hair is a shimmering mop of an unruly mess, and his irises appear to have been painted with the most enticing, darkened pools of a beautiful deep violet. Each long lashed eye is flecked with what I can only describe as something that reminds me of small pieces of precious gold leaf.

He's now curling his tongue over his upper lip and I am immediately drawn to his curvaceous mouth. I find myself wondering what it would feel like to press my lips to his. I am awoken from my sensuous thoughts when he places his hand over mine and slowly removes my fork from between my trembling fingers. As we momentarily touch, the sheer charge of electricity that flows over my skin is verging on the unbearable. Shuddering at the feel of his warmth that is emanating from his being, I am instantly mesmerized as the sound of the cutlery passes through the cube and jangles on the plate. Placing the prongs to my lips, he grins and softly urges, "Go on, be a brave girl and taste it for me."

Rooted to the spot at the sheer audacity of this man, I can't even open my mouth to tell him to go away, let alone eat the damn cube!

"Well, are you going to open your mouth for me or am I going to have to eat it for you?" he teases.

Still unable to move, my eyes widen as he leans in towards me, opens his mouth and seductively curls his lips around the morsel. The moving image right in front of me and the scent of his manliness is enough to leave me breathless. Removing the utensil from his mouth, he places it back on my plate, swallows his mouthful and chuckles, "Well, Ms, you missed out there. It *was* rather delicious."

Leaving me with my mouth agape, he winks at me, licks his lips, turns on his heel and struts off. Watching him intently, I frown as he perches himself on the arm of the sofa that is situated against the back wall and shoots me another thigh-squeezing gorgeous lash bat. Picking up a magazine from the table, he flicks through it, and without looking upwards, he then proceeds to begin a conversation with the woman sitting next to him. Tossing the glossy print down, he grasps her hand, upturns it and begins to stroke her palm. That was when I felt a peculiar stab of jealousy hit me right in the gut. I had to get out of here. I really did, before I did something I knew I could possibly regret later. Making it to the sidewalk, I pause and fumble in my bag for my car keys. Muttering to myself that in the future I must try to be more organised with the contents of my bag, I am distracted from my task when I hear a soft voice...

"Sorry," it whispers, "I am really sorry for teasing you back there. Please would you consider turning around and letting me apologise to you properly?"

Feeling the anger rising in me, I knew if I did turn around one of two things could happen. I would either introduce him to one of my now legendary slaps for his pure cheekiness or I would launch myself at him in the hope of being on the receiving end of a lingering kiss. In such a sexy tone, his voice thawing me a little, he asks me if I am always this stubborn.

Yes I am I think to myself. Unlocking my car, I take a deep breath and decide it would be best all-round if I ignore him. Anyway, why was he even here? Shouldn't he be with his girlfriend? My hands are now shaking and I accidently drop my keys to the kerb. Bending down to pick them up, he beats me to it, scoops them up and tightly curls his fist around them. He removes his sunglasses and that is when our eyes lock. A thousand burning, enticing sensations surge through my body at an alarming rate and as he waves his hand in the air and teases, he says, "Kiss me and then you can have them back." Glancing around, he then laughs, "Go on, I dare you! I can assure you no one's looking!"

He tilts his head to one side and childishly pleads with me for just one fleeting kiss. I have to close my eyes so I can blot out the sensual bows of his lips. As the silent moments pass by, eventually I find my voice, open my eyes and sarcastically retort, "Look, I don't know who you are and neither do I care. You are just making my bad day even worse. Now I suggest you give me back my keys and go and find your girlfriend. I guess the poor woman is wondering where her scheming boyfriend has sloped off to!"

Reeling back from me, he stuffs his hands into his jeans pockets, slumps his shoulders and breathes, "Sorry, Ms. I am really truly sorry. I didn't mean to upset you. Please accept my sincerest and most humble of apologies." Walking away from me, he then turns and chuckles,

"Oh by the way, Ms. she's not my girlfriend, she's just a family friend. And just in case you are wondering, my name is Theo."

I was speculating as to his name…

CHAPTER THREE

Shoving my cell into my sweatpants pockets, I grab my iPod, and since it was a cool spring morning here in London, I decided a jog around my local park would help to erase Theo from my mind. Slamming my flat door shut, I head for the elevator. Reaching the foyer, I step out and head for the exit. Holding the door open for me was our usual cheery doorman.

"Good morning, Eden," he gaily chirps.

"And a good morning to you, Ellis."

Tipping his hat to me, he smiles and informs me that it is a beautiful day for me to breathe in the scented spring air whilst enjoying my daily run. I smile and tell him that I will. Plugging in to my system, I avert my gaze from my choice of music, glance upwards, and it as at that point – when my vision falls upon the car parked directly in front of me, that my heart almost misses a vital beat. There he is in all his cocky glory, lounging across the passenger seat of his Audi Cabriolet, dressed in full business attire, holding a bunch of lilac and white flowers that were interspaced with green foliage – and just to make me melt even further, he is grinning at me like the cat who had just had a sneaky taste of the delicious forbidden cream from the top of a recently delivered doorstep milk bottle.

Oh, that rather infectious smile of his!

Before I had a chance to put one foot forward, he leaps over the side of the car, paces towards me, gets down on one knee and proceeds to tell me he is sorry for his flirty behaviour yesterday and if there was anything he can to do to make up for it, he will. I just couldn't help but burst out laughing at this rather ridiculous scenario. Him down on one knee with a rather over-the-top display of flowers... Me, standing here in full jogging attire... Heaven knows what Ellis thought, let alone any of the morning passers-by. He breaks the ice by gazing up me and smiling. "I know what you're thinking," he chortles, "you're thinking everyone who can see us thinks I am asking you to marry me!"

I couldn't help it. I really couldn't help teasing him. I did owe him a quick retort for his boldness. The words just tumbled out of my mouth without any warning. "Well, are you, Theo?"

Rising to his feet, he drops the flowers to his side. Taking a step closer, he leans in towards me, takes a deep sigh and in such a hushed tone, he murmurs into my ear, "Do you want me to, Eden?"

My knees now weakening, he senses this and steadies me by boldly snaking his free hand around my waist. Feeling the heat of his person penetrating through my thin vest only causes me to falter further. Locking gazes, he creases a frown and declares, "I want you, Eden. I want every part of you."

I am now so totally mesmerised by his piercing eyes, his plump lips and his delightful, freshly-laundered linen scent that I don't even consider using my common sense to ask him how he knew where I lived or how he knew my name. Letting the bouquet fall to the pavement, he brings his hand towards my cheek and lightly skims my cheekbone with his finger, and in such an innocent, childlike tone he tenderly asks if he can kiss me. I can't reply because I am completely and utterly mesmerized by this man's aura. There is something almost so inexperienced that hides within the sweet undertones of his voice, but at the same time, he exudes a magnetic charm that I find I am fast becoming drawn to. So with all this new information infiltrating my mind, I just stand rooted to the spot, feeling as giddy as a schoolgirl who had yet to experience her first kiss from her promised first love. Pushing a little more into me, he breathes, "Shall take your silence as a yes?"

I nod in acceptance. I do this because I quite simply fear that if I spoke, 'no' might fall from my lips, and then I may never get the chance again to be this close to him.

Surprising me by lightly kissing me on the tip of my nose instead of my lips, he removes his hands from me and asks if I would dine with him this evening. Bending down, he scoops up the flowers and offers them to me. I take them from him and I shock us both by mumbling a rather weak, 'No.'

He doesn't question me; he just stuffs his hands in his trouser pockets, shrugs his shoulders and mumbles, "If that is what you wish, Eden."

He turns on his heal. My mouth is now a-gape and as I watch him amble towards his car, I want to shout out for him to stop and tell him that I will have dinner with him but he didn't give me a backward glance. I desperately wanted him to turn around but he just leapt in his car, started up the engine and drove off at a rather fast speed. I guess that was that. Until three weeks later…

CHAPTER FOUR

Stepping out of the elevator, I gasp out loud when I see the young man leaning up against my apartment door. There he is again. *My mischievous Theo.*

He is casually leaning on the door… His hair is a sexy mess of blond, gorgeous curls and I can't help but imagine what it would be like to run my fingers through each of his silky spirals. He glances up at me and beams me the most heart-stopping smile. I find myself blushing and my face reddens even further when I see him hook his thumbs in the top of his jeans, and I shiver inside when I realise that the first few buttons are undone. He shimmies them down so they just rest on his hips and I have to roll my eyes to the left, because all the evidence I see indicates to me that this man is naked beneath the soft ripped denim that clinging to his muscular thighs. Trying my hardest not to show him that I am not only amazed at his boldness but that I am also secretly pleased to see him, I sigh and ask him what he is doing here. In such a honeyed tone, he drawls, "I told you before, Eden. I want you to have dinner with me."

I nervously laugh and ask him if he wouldn't mind moving away from my door. He shifts a little to the left, and as I approach him, he gently grasps my wrist and draws me into him. I miss a breath as he tips his finger under my chin and tilts my face so I have no choice but to see his stunning eyes.

"There's nowhere for you go, Eden. Nowhere for you to run except into my bed."

I swallow hard. His sheer sexiness combined with his persistence in shadowing me is unnerving me, but at the same time they both excite me.

He bows down to me and brushes his lips along mine. "You want me as much as I want you, don't you?"

I cannot resist him any longer. His manly fragrance is sending me giddy. I haven't seen him since the day he gave me flowers, and I must admit I have thought about him every day since then… and now, here in the hallway to my apartment, he's finally snared me and I think I am just about ready to play the game with him.

"Yes, I… I…"

I don't get a chance to finish my sentence because I am distracted by the movement of his hands, and as they brush along my tummy, I point my lashes down to see what he is doing. I focus upon his fingers and nervously chew the corner of my bottom lip because the teasing imp is slowly buttoning up his jeans!

"Stop looking at my groin," he chuckles, "and would you please try to act like a lady and look at my face instead."

I dreamily gaze back up at him and my heart flips when he beams like a Cheshire cat and questions, "You didn't think I was going to wall-bang you here did you?"

I am so frustrated by this tease of his that I pull away from him and retort, "You didn't think I was going to degrade myself by letting you?"

Silent moments pass and as I go to repeat my question, we both fall into fits of raucous laughter. Tucking his tee into his jeans, he cocks his head to one side, grins and asks if I would have dinner with him. Once again I shock us both by replying, 'No'.

I didn't see him again until four days later.

CHAPTER FIVE

Finishing painting my last toenail my favourite electric blue colour, I am distracted by a knock at the door. Quizzing as to why Ellis hadn't buzzed me to tell me someone was on their way up, I hoped that the unannounced visitor might be my best friend, Jules. Jules was an artist; well, he was a struggling artist who took great pleasure in dabbling with canvas and oils. Some of his work even though abstract was quite intriguing to say the least. He was full of fun and laughter and right now I could do with cheering up after this morning's disastrous encounter with *my mischievous Theo*.

As the knock became more urgent, I screwed the cap back on the bottle and hollered that I was coming.

"Jules, calm down, I'm nearly with you," I blurt.

Flinging the door open, not looking up as I was checking to see if my toenail polish had dried, I laugh, "What's so urgent that you have to virtually hammer my door to death, my baby boy?"

The voice I hear throws me off. It's recently become a familiar, honeyed, amusing tone and I instantly know who it belongs to.

"Well, Eden, how delightful of you to call me your baby boy! I'm rather touched by your words!" it exclaims "And don't you just look stunning wrapped in a silk kimono with dripping wet hair and blue... um are they blue toenails you have?"

Glancing up as I see Theo, I try to speak. He raises his palm as if to silence me, half-grins, holds up a picnic basket and cheekily suggests, "I like silk very much, especially on you, and I love blue toenails for that matter. I could kiss each one of your pretty little toes!"

I gulp at the thought of him on his knees seductively sucking each toe in turn while I writhe under his touch.

He continues, "And since you refused to have dinner with me twice, I decided to bring dinner to you! You do like feta cheese, don't you?" he chortles.

Cheeky devil!

Unaware that I was openly biting the corner of my lip again, I shudder as he taps me lightly on the tip of my nose and whispers, "Eden, you appear to be daydreaming and by the way, you are chewing your lip. I assume it must be a rather erotic thought."

He was right! This is exactly what I was thinking:

I want him to kiss me, and I crave to feel his warm breath infuse into my mouth, combined with the soft strokes of his fingers as they skim down the back of my spine and rest just above the dip at the top of my buttocks... It's the split second that follows, when he whispers into my ear what he wants to do to me, that makes me inpatient. I grasp his wrist and place his hands between my legs, softly urging him to caress my sensitive spot. When he does, my mind screams, lower, softer... lick me lightly there… make me cum with your tongue… He reads my mind and instantly sinks to his knees…

"Eden, wake up," he whispers, "come back to earth, my dear lady. I need you on this planet because we have lots to achieve together in the future."

On hearing him say 'in the future', I propel myself back to earth, open my mental parachute, land back on my virtual feet and squeak, "What on earth are you doing here?"

He offers me the basket, and I don't know why, but I automatically take it from him. Next, he angles his head to one side, smiles in a triumphant fashion and quickly brushes past me.

"Excuse me," I exclaim, "you didn't answer my question, and exactly where do you think you are going?"

"I'm going to your kitchen. Is that all right with you?"

I grumble a *yes* and push the front door to whilst coming to the conclusion that sharing a picnic with him won't hurt. Once we've eaten, I'll send him on his merry way. I will consider this evening just a bit of fun. Catching him up, I inform him that the kitchen is through the door right in front of him.

He nudges the door open, and in a firm tone, he thanks me and tells me to go and find some wine glasses while he uncorks a bottle of wine. Setting two glasses down on the work station, I watch him pull out a bottle and corkscrew from the basket and expertly uncork. Pouring us both a glass, he looks up at me. Taking a sip of his drink, he seductively licks his lips. By that suggestive gesture of his, I now find myself beginning to spiral out of control. Then, out of the blue, he states, "Before I leave tonight, Eden, I *am* going to kiss you."

I pick up my glass and turn my back to him. He's really unnerving me now, so I stare into the red liquid, take a deep breath, and as I place the rim of the glass to my lips – before I could even take my first taste of a much needed courage – I feel a light kiss settle upon the back of my neck. As the hairs on my flesh erect and tingle from the softness of his lips, I instantly drop my glass. It falls to the floor and shatters into shards.

He snakes his arms around my waist, gives me a gentle squeeze and orders me not to move. I'm stunned! Scooping me up into his arms, he skirts around the broken pieces and gaily asks, "Where's your bedroom?"

Oh my, why does he want to know where my bedroom is? I gulp at the thought of him in my boudoir. My head is now in a total spin. Do I tell him where my room is? And if I do, do I take the lead and entice him into my bed?

"Um... Straight ahead," I stutter, "it's... it's... the door to the left."

He struts towards the door and nudges it open with his foot. Walking towards my unmade bed, he plants a kiss upon the tip of my nose and suggests that I should go and get dressed, because he would find it rather distracting trying to eat dinner with me if I remained in my kimono. Exiting my room, he doesn't turn around, he just shouts, "And while you're dressing, I will clean up the glass. Please don't be long, Eden. We have lots to discuss and I still want a kiss before I leave you tonight."

I am now in a total state of shock. What is this man doing to me? And more so, why is he even *here* in my apartment? I fling off my gown and go on the hunt for the safety of my jeans…

~ ~ ~

Returning from the bedroom, I walk through the kitchen and smile when I see that he has not only cleaned up the mess but he has also poured me a fresh glass of wine. I pick up my drink and gingerly peek around the kitchen door, with the full intent of spying on him a little. Seeing him splayed out on my sofa, looking so damn sexy and casually sipping away, I gasp out a little too loudly. He rises his head on hearing me, beams the sweetest of smile and places his glass down onto the coffee table. Not only does he look so sexy wearing a tight black tee and matching jeans but the way he's draped his taut body over the cushions, languishing as if it was a regular occurrence to be in my home makes me call out to him and enquire if he always made a habit of making himself comfortable in strangers' homes.
He skims his bottom lip with the pad of his thumb, crosses his legs and cheekily replies, "Always… I always do!"

Patting the cushions, he then suggests it would be nice if I came and sat next to him. I decline. Instead I walk to the armchair opposite him and seat myself there. On seeing me cross my legs, he jests, "You should've worn a short skirt instead of jeans! I'm curious to see your bare, long legs!"

Trying to stifle an impending giggle, I tut-tut him and smile sweetly while offering, "Jeans are a safer item of clothing to wear, especially when you're around, Theo!"

Quietness hangs in the air for the briefest of moments, and when we have both regained our composures, I take a breath and decide it's time for some serious talk. I have so many questions for him and I want answers to all of them before I make the decision as to whether I want or – whether I need –someone like him in my life.

"So, tell me, Theo, how do you know my name?"

Circling the rim of his glass with his finger, he muses for a while and says, "The restaurant we were in the other night, my brother owns it. So I saw you, thought you were rather cute and decided I wanted you. I checked the reservations list – and voila! I know your name."

Now opening giggling at the fact he thought I was rather cute, he asks me what is so amusing. I take another sip; ignore his question and move on to my next one. Watching him uncross his legs, my gaze automatically homes in on his rather impressive groin.

Stop it, Eden, my sub-conscious whispers, *stop ogling him.*

"How did you know where I live?"

He fixes his gaze on me, and in an almost embarrassed fashion he informs me that two nights ago he followed me home from the restaurant. Raising his palm as if to apprehend me from speaking, he rises from the sofa and walks towards me. I can feel the charge rampantly gaining momentum within the room. It's becoming positively electrifying and as the adrenaline pours into my bloodstream, my heart begins to race. He's now standing directly in front of me. "Give me your hand, Eden," he orders. I do.

He pulls me up, places both my arms around his neck and snakes his arms around my waist. We are so close that I can feel his manhood pressing into me and I know that if I weaken now, I won't be able to stop myself from devouring him in one foul swoop. He starts to gently nip the side of my neck, while murmuring, *"I am forever at your service. I will always be at your beck and call."*

I'm dwindling at his words… I don't resist against him. How could I? This man is positively divine with his smouldering good looks and graceful stature. He's every woman's dream and the way he is tentatively pushing his hardness into me is making it rather difficult for me to ignore him. I swear he should be considered 'an illegal property'. He's now staring at me hard. No words need to be spoken; at this particular moment in time our eyes are sharing the same vocabulary. They are dancing with their own magical twenty-six letters of the alphabet. We are so close to each other and I'm trying so hard to resist crushing my lips to his. I mustn't take the lead this time. If I do, I will fail. I always flop in matters of the heart.

"I'm going to kiss you now, Eden. Do you want me too?"

I can't answer him. I am transfixed by his presence. His lips are hovering above mine and his sexy, husky voice keeps asking me over and over, *do you want me*. He so tenderly cups my face in his hands and whispers, "Are you ready, Eden?"

I nod and his lips finally settle upon mine. He prises my mouth open with his tongue and the warmth, the sweet taste and the teasing slight of it as he darts it in and out of mine transforms into a hedonistic trio of sensuality that can only ever be created by him for me. Not only is each one of his kisses brimming with a deep, yearning passion for me, everyone that he is bestowing upon me is rapidly turning into a silent statement of his undying love. Every breath that I feel of his upon my lips is causing me to waiver even further. He's now steadying my face in his strong hands, and while his eyelids flutter, he presses his mouth to mine. Our lips collide and the sensuous kiss he bestows upon me is so divine to say the least. The warmth – the taste of his tongue dipping with mine – is enough to liquefy me. Quite simply, he has me and there is not a thing I can do to stave off the feelings that are now racing through my body and soul. He's kissing me in such a way that one would've thought he had been starved of love for centuries. Something's reawakening in me and I feel as if I am being coaxed out from a deep sleep, much like sleeping beauty that was doomed to slumber for a hundred years.

His kisses are the type that I had only ever dreamt about in my wildest fantasies. No man until now had ever made me feel so desired, so needed and so beautiful all at the same time.

He opens his eyes and the lustful gaze that pours from his soul and into mine is one of an apparition. It's as if he has been struck by a radiant, magical beauty that has laid open her soul to him... and with each of the tender following kisses he bestows upon me, every one that falls from his lips and settles upon mine, every *single one* made me feel like *his* enchanting princess.

"You all right, Eden?" he softly asks. "You seem to be lost."

I am.

I don't answer him. I just run my fingers through his silky curls, press my lips to his and relish in dancing my tongue around his. He stuns me by pulling away and bowing his head. An uncomfortable aura immediately surrounds us and I begin to feel… *confused.*

"What's the matter?" I ask. "Look up at me, Theo. Please look up at me."

He raises his head, and as I see the teary glaze in his eyes, I reach out for him, but he takes a step back from me. I shudder and ask, "What is it? What have I done? Have I upset you in any way?"

After a long pause, he finally speaks. "You haven't done anything wrong. It's just that I felt something so powerful, so stirring within our kiss that I can't help but want to make love to you right now. I want us to get lost in each-other's souls."

~ ~ ~

THEO'S THOUGHTS

She's just simply breathtaking… She's consuming me with her deep, extracting kisses. She's pulling out every ounce of emotion from me, and the passion that's flowing from her lips, her tongue and her soul sends me spiralling into another dimension. When she whispers my name, it scampers through my mind conjuring up images only I will ever know… I am now immersed in her aura and I don't ever want to be submerged back into the harsh, cruel reality of life.

~ ~ ~

I take a tentative step towards him. Relief floods over me as, this time, he shows no sign of moving away. I offer him my hand and he takes it in his. I give it a light squeeze and ask, "You feel that strongly about me? You're talking about making love and finding souls?"

"Yes, I do." He sighs. "I want to make love to you, but first I want to be a true gentleman and date you."

I entwine my fingers with his, pull him closer to me and tell him that that is what I would like too.

He closes his eye-lids, lets out another sigh and then murmurs, "I'm hungry, Eden. All that kissing has made me rather ravenous, and my hunger is not only for you and your body, but for food too!"

I start giggling at his words, and his eyelids flick open. The dreamy look that's exuding from his sparkling irises is enough to make me fall head-over-heels in love with him. Yes, there, I finally admit to myself… *I am not only in love with this man, I am positively awestruck, and I know that I am never going to be able to extract him from under my skin. I don't want to, because he is mine, he always will be and I am his.*

CHAPTER SIX

"Where are we going, Theo?" I ask.

Not taking his vision off the road, he tells me it's a surprise and I will just have to wait and see.

Leaning back into the passenger seat, I close my eyes only to instantly open them as I feel his hand push my silk skirt up over my knee and brush against my garter. Glancing over at him, he breaks into an impish smile and places his hand back on the steering wheel. The gentleness of his touch only serves to make me want another, so I breathe, "I wish you'd touch me again, Theo."

He doesn't respond to my request; he just keeps driving. Halting at a set of traffic lights, he turns to face me and as I see the dewy look in his stunning eyes, my heart flips. "I want you too, Eden," he whispers. "I want to kiss you right now."

What is this man doing to me? I don't think I shall be able to resist him much longer, so I tell him that even though I want him too, I would like him to stop tempting me.

The lights change to green, he hits the accelerator and laughs. "Okay, I'll behave if you will!"

Don't do it, Eden, my subconscious orders, *don't you dare do what I think you're going to do!*

I ignore her… She's beginning to annoy me of late.

I chose to ignore *her*, place my hand upon his thigh, give him a gentle squeeze and let my palm rest there for a moment. The firmness of his taut muscle as it twitches instantly takes my breath away. He responds by a hitching breath, and as a gasp escapes his lips I lean into him and whisper what I would like to do to him in the car. He carries on driving without saying a word until the moment he finds a safe place to stop.

Pulling over onto the grass verge, he switches off the engine, unbuckles both our seat belts and without giving me a split second to react, he presses his lips to mine and murmurs, "Even though I desperately want you, Eden, I don't want the first time we make love to be in my car. Cars are for driving in – and sometimes if one is too horny and can't wait for a release, they can be used for fucking purposes."

Pulling back from me, he gently grabs my hand and takes my palm. Stroking my flesh in such a sensual way, the lightness of his touch and the softness of the sensation of his leather glove as it skims my skin sends shivers down my spine and then in a beautiful, soft voice, he declares, "I don't just want you, Eden. I told you that before. I want much more than that. I desire a long, slow, sweet session of passionate love making with you, and I want that beautiful act to occur in my bed. A haven where we can devour each other's bodies in all manner of ways… This is one of the many ways that I wish to pleasure *us*… Do you want to hear it?"

By the glint in his eyes and the way he's smirking, I think he knows that he has me intrigued, so I that tell him I do. He smiles, gazes into my eyes and then blinds me with his words of sheer, unadulterated honesty. "I want to introduce you and your body to the highest, sexual plane imaginable. I want to see the glazed look in your eyes as I make you cum over and over again for me. I want to sit back and take delight in seeing you when your body is a quivering heap of a sweaty mess and your thighs are trembling from sheer exhaustion."

My mouth now agape, he creases a frown, pauses and asks me if I would like to hear what else he would like to do to me. I am so captivated by watching his lips move and his tongue flick over his lower lip that I just nod in approval. Strangely, he blushes, curls his fingers tighter around mine, takes a deep breath and declares, "I also want to cum for you in multiple ways. Firstly I want make love to you. I want to make slow, sweet, gentle love to you and I want to revel in hearing you call out my name when we orgasm together. Secondly, I want you to make me cum in your hand. I want to see the look in your eyes as you slowly work my cock until I explode… and I want to see the look on your face when I release and drench your fingers in an abundance of my warm, precious fluid.

A quivering, "Oh" is all that I can manage to rise from my now-squeaking voice.

He beams a mischievous grin and tells me that he hasn't finished describing how he wants to pleasure me, so without hesitation, he continues.

"I also desire to release into your sweet, warm mouth, but before that pleasure, I want to relish in the moment when I see your eyelids flicker when you feel my fluid flowing over your heated skin, and as I trail the last few drops of my hot opaque offering down your slender neck, I want to see your hand slip between your thighs and hear you groan as you tease yourself until I ask you if you would like me to make love to you again."

Oh my, he's so hot with words!

"I also want to lie on your chest and listen to your heartbeat as it returns to its regular rhythm and when it does, I will start all over again, exciting you, and I wish to begin this by introducing you to a blindfold."

With his bold declarations, he has instantly turned me into a mute. I am so blown away by his statement that all I can do is continue to stare at him in amazement. Now stroking my hand, he softly pleads with me to speak to him. I finally find my voice. It waivers a little but I manage to respond, "Theo, you sound like a man who has had so much experience in these matters. May I ask if you have?"

Instantly, he releases my hand and mutters for me to buckle up because he no longer wants to take me to his favourite restaurant, he want us to be alone to talk so therefore we are going back to his house. I don't know why but I sense that he is suddenly overcome with embarrassment, so I do as he asks. As he drives, I mull over his words. I have never in my entire life heard a man speak so bluntly – so honestly – about either the way he feels about me or about what he desires to do in the sexual department.

He senses this, I'm sure of that, so we travel in silence to his home. I'm pleased that we are quiet because it will give me time to continue digesting his rather honest and erotic thoughts.

CHAPTER SEVEN

As the headlights of his car illuminate the driveway, I see in the distance the most stunning modern building in front of us. It can't possibly be his home, could it?

"Is this your home, Theo?"

He pulls up alongside the front of the house, draws to a halt and switches of the engine. He doesn't reply. He just unbuckles my seat belt and tells me to stay in my seat. I do as he requests because I am still reeling from this whole bizarre situation. He comes around to my side of the car and opens the door for me. Extending his hand to me, I place my palm in his hand and, once again I shiver at the feel of the soft animal skin as it brushes against my skin.

"Come on, Eden." In such a child-like fashion, he gaily chirps, "I want to show you inside my home."

Holding my hand tight, he guides me towards the door and punches in a code. I can't believe what I see. Said door opens on its own.

"Wow!" I gasp. "That's pretty amazing."

He chuckles and tells me that's his latest fun gadget. He walks me inside and I draw a breath as I see the hallway. We are now in what I can only describe as the most ornate foyer I have seen. The floor is pristine white marble and the white walls just make the entrance look almost clinical. He flings his keys into the bowl that nestles on the table, removes his gloves and tosses them over onto his keys. Turning to face me he smiles and asks, "So what do you think of my house so far? Do you like it?"

I smile back and tell him that so far I think it's *rather* beautiful. He nods in approval and tells me to follow him. I am now so intrigued by him that I find myself dying to ask him what he does for a living. I follow him down the hallway and pass through a set of already opened French doors. I stop when I see the room in front of me. It's so vast; I swear that you could just live in this space alone.

"This is your kitchen?"

"Yup!" he chuckles. "It sure is. Can you cook, Eden, because I am rather ravenous?"

I start laughing because this man is so damn cheeky and one just has to love him solely for that cutest of attributes.

"What's so funny?"

"You… This … *Us*…"

He leans into me and tells me he liked the way I said 'us'. It makes him feel complete.

Oh, what is this man doing to me? I barely know him and he's already capturing fragments of my heart. He then suggests that if I can't cook, we can always get take-out, or if I wasn't hungry, we could go over to the workstation situated in the centre of the room and make love there!

I swat him away and giggle, "Is that all you ever think about, Theo, sex?"

The glint in his eyes tells me he probably does. He pulls out a bar stool and I sit down. I watch him as he strides over to the fridge and stands motionless in front of it. After a few moments he asks me if I'd like white wine to drink or would I prefer a glass of champagne. I choose the latter. Now sitting opposite each other, he pours us both a flute, offers me a glass, takes a sip of his and then asks me if I would like to know what he does for work. I take a sip of mine and tell him that I would. In such a matter-of-fact tone he tells me that he is a CEO of his own company. I splutter on my drink and blurt it out so it spills down my chin. He tuts in disgust at my display of un-ladylike manners and opens the draw situated next to him. Withdrawing a crisp white linen folded napkin, he shakes it out and quietly whispers, "I think I had better dab that liquid off your face rather quickly because the way it's trailing down your pretty face is making me have uncontrollable desire to lick it off!"

I go stiff at his words. The thought of him licking champagne off my face rapidly transpires into erotic thoughts of him pouring it over my naked body and trailing his tongue...

As he dabs away he asks, "Why is so funny to you that I am CEO?"

I giggle and say it isn't. It is just that he totally surprised me with his answer and that I have a penchant for powerful, sexy men who steal the feta cheese off my plate and then proceed to seductively eat it. He shakes his head from side-to-side and sighs at my answer. I then ask him what his work entails. He sets the napkin down, hops off the stool and walks towards the door we came through.

"Come on, bring your drink and we can sit in the lounge. It's more comfortable in there."

~ ~ ~

We sit opposite each other on the sofa. He smiles so sweetly at me and then informs me of what he does for a living.

"I am a software developer."

"You mean you are a geek who cracks codes and puts gremlins into computers," I tease.

He furrows his brow, chews the corner of his lip and sighs. "That's what most people think of me but no, my love, I am not a geek who does those things. I am in fact a genius."

We both fall into hysterics and he surprises me when he says he thinks we will be good together because we both share a similar sense of humour. I have to agree with him. We do!

"Theo?" I ask, "Why are you single? You are so handsome, so intelligent and I would imagine that you would have women falling at your feet."

He creases another worried frown, and for a moment I think I have may have overstepped the mark. Shuffling up towards me, he takes my hands in his and breathes, "Eden, that is such a beautiful description of how you see me. I am truly touched by your words and I will tell you why I am single. I have not met a woman who I want to share my body and soul with yet."

I withdraw my hands from his and my heart sinks at his blunt honesty. I refrain from asking him if I could be the right woman for him. After all, he's just told me that I am not the one, hasn't he?

"I think I had better go home Theo," I weakly offer, "If you just want me as a plaything like the woman I saw you with in the restaurant, then I am sorry, because that is not the way I wish to conduct my life."

A look of pure horror spreads across his face and I can't fathom what on earth is going on. He lunges at me, nearly knocking me off the sofa, and bats his lashes and cups my face in his hands.

"No… No… my darling Eden," he exclaims. "That is most definitely not what I meant to say."

He steadies my face in his now-trembling hands and brushes a lone tear that somehow worked its way free from my soul without any warning. I try to pull away but he won't let me, so instead I close my eyes. "Eden… Look at me."

I can't for fear that if I do, I will melt right into his beautiful soul.

"Well, if you won't look at me then hear this – I want *you* to be my girlfriend. You are the one—" he so soulfully declares. A brief silence fills the air only to be broken by the sound of his voice in a lower meltier tone— that I want to share my body and soul with. Do you understand me?"

On hearing his words, I instantly open my eyes. He's now grinning like a child who's pleased his mother by achieving a top grade at school.

"You want what? You want to do what with me?"

"Do you want me to spell it out for you?"

He's now running his fingers along my side, and as he reaches just below my breast, he slides his hand over my bare back and rests his palm upon my skin. Brushing his lips along mine, he groans, "Your skin is so soft, so warm. I want to…"

He stops and then asks, "Do you wish me to tell you exactly what I mean when I said you are the one?"

I nod. I desperately need to hear his honest declaration.

"I've fallen in love with you, Eden. It's as simple as that. I've never felt like this before about any woman. These feelings that are running through me are so strong, so powerful that not only am I constantly weak at the knees for you, I am also honoured you helped me discover the passion that has lain dormant within my soul for far too long... and that beautiful four-lettered word *love*… because of you… I now have come to understand the meaning of"— He pauses— "and it was at the moment when you walked into my world that it hit me… Your entirety is and always will be the true definition of the meaning of love."

This man has just left me breathless with his honesty. I am now somewhere else. My mind is a whirl and I find myself lost within an abundance of his slow, calming kisses... We kiss for what seems forever, until we both have to pull away to regain some sort of unspoken composure. As I open my eyelids and focus upon him, I'm so touched by the sensitivity that surrounds him because this specimen of a sexy creature is openly blushing before my very eyes.

He stands up and changes the whole ambience by asking me to stay seated and sip on my champagne. He informs me that he won't be long because he has to make a business phone call. I should find it odd that in the midst of our passion, he decides to think business, but considering the way he looked after our shared kisses, I come to the conclusion that maybe he needs to compile and clarify his thoughts. He disappears out of the door and I take the moment to scan the room. As I do, my vision falls upon a lone photograph that stands upon the grand piano situated in the far corner of the room. I walk over and pick it up. My heart flips when I see Theo in an embrace with a svelte, blonde lady dressed in a gold evening dress. She is stunningly beautiful to say the least. Her bare back is slightly arched and she is being supported by his muscular arms. The way he's cradling her is one of a look of protectiveness. She is gazing up at him and the glaze cast in her eyes is one of an undoubtable deep, unashamed love.

She loves my Theo

I stare at it for what seems like ages, until I hear his voice across the room. His tone is firm but of a fairish manner and I am ordered to put the photograph back down. I turn around and blink. In fact I have to double-take because he has changed out of his suit and is wearing the same pair of ripped, faded jeans that he teased me with before... and nothing else. I try to catch my breath at seeing his naked torso for the first time. A light splattering of fair, curly hair tumbles down his chest and every muscle that radiates from his centre is so finely tuned to the hilt that I could easily count them from where I am standing. I look down his legs until I reach his bare feet. I am in serious trouble now because this man is so hot, so sexy and so damn enticing that I try to push the photograph to the back of my mind and concentrate on whether I should let my guard down even further and become one with him.

His tone lightens and he gently orders me to come over and meet him on the sofa. I quickly place the frame back on the piano in fear of dropping it from my shaking hand. He lies down upon the leather and places a cushion behind his head. He drapes his body in such a suggestive manner over the length of the sofa that the aching that's increasing between my dampening centre informs me that it has now become impossible to resist him. On reaching him, he extends his hand to me.

I take it and bravely ask, "Who is the woman in the photograph, Theo? You both seemed to be very much in love."

He yanks me onto him, and as I straddle him, he cups me around the back of my head and we are now face-to-face. He kisses the tip of my nose and breathes, "She is my dance partner. She has been since we were twelve years old – her name is Charlotte."

"Oh! I exclaim, I thought…"

He places his finger to my lips, presses it lightly, shushes me and laughs. "I know what you thought; you thought she was my girlfriend, didn't you? And you went into a bit of downer considering that I had only moments ago told you that I have fallen for you. You began to question if I was telling you the truth about my feelings. Well let me assure you of this – I am!"

Now it's my turn to blush. "I'm sorry, Theo. Yes I did. You just looked so in love with each other."

"Ah", he exclaims, "that's the beautiful power of music – it can transport you to anywhere when you least expect it to."

The conversation ends there and the physical starts to take over. I am now sitting on top of him and he is untying the back of my halter-neck top. As the straps release, it slips down, revealing the tops of my breast. His body responds by his cock twitching against my thigh. "Hell, Eden," he gasps, "you are just so beautiful and sexy. I think we are going to have to go upstairs and finish this in my bed."

I smile and nod. I'm now yearning to be tangled between the sheets with him – to be lost within the deep throes of passion, and I for one don't want us to be found, but I wish to excite a little first, so I skim my fingers across his bare, taut chest and tentatively linger my palm over what appears to be a recently small black-inked heart-shaped tattoo that is imprinted upon his gently heaving left breast. I move my hand an inch further over and lightly rest it upon the precious place where his heart beats. The strong metronomic rhythm of his thumping lifeline only serves to heighten my sexual desire for him further. I kiss him in the hollow of his shoulder and he takes a sharp intake of breath when my lips connect with his warm, scented flesh. He's now titling his head backwards and his breathing is becoming more apparent. I can't make out what he murmurs to me, so I let my other hand skim over the top of his jeans. As my fingers locate the top button, I begin to undo the first, then the second. His hardness is now straining against the soft ripped denim and I for one wish to free it from its tight restraint. I slide down his body, planting sweet, little peppery kisses all over his chest until he shudders and asks me to stop. "Please, baby," he groans, "please let me take you upstairs. I want to make love to you for the first time in the comfort of my bed."

He rolls us both onto the floor, and as my back hits the floor I let out a little yelp. His face crumples and he starts planting delicate kisses upon my forehead while murmuring, "Have I hurt you? Please tell me I haven't hurt you."

I angle my hips up towards him and push my body into him. "No, you haven't hurt me. It was just a bit of a shock." And what did he mean by 'I want to make love to you for the first time in the comfort of my bed'? Does he mean he has never made love before or does he mean the 'first' time of many love-making sessions that will follow?

"Phew," he sighs with relief and then mischievously chuckles, "do you want to see my bedroom?"

"I do," I giggle, "but first, will you tell me why you have a fresh tattoo inked on your chest?"

He takes a deep sign and flops flat onto his back. I roll onto my side, prop myself up on my elbow and try not to focus on the bulge in his groin but the sensuous curves of his lips. I run my finger around the circumference of the heart tattoo and he then proceeds to tell me why.

"When I first saw you in the restaurant, that was the day I went and had it done. I figured that if I never saw you again, at least I would have a piece of your heart close to mine."

A few moments of silence pass and I find my voice. "You had that done because of me?" I whisper. "You really do feel that passionate towards me?"

He rolls back over to face me, and when I see the adorable look of innocence exuding from his eyes, I melt. When taps his tattoo, he flinches a little at the sensitivity of it and breathes, "You will always be in my heart, my soul and my life. I will love you, Eden, for eternity and if there is anything beyond that, then I will love you in that most mystical and magical of secret places."

Oh.

He shuffles onto his knees and rises to his feet. Extending his arm to me, I take his hand and he curls his fingers around mine. Helping me to my feet, he smiles and then whisks me up into his arms. Nuzzling my nose with his, he purrs, "I'm taking you upstairs now. I want us to shower together. I want us to intimately wash each other."

I can't utter a single word because while he's carrying me forth, he is planting delicate, soft kisses upon my lips and I am feeling so loved, so cosseted by him that I have without question, just at this moment, silently bequeathed my soul to him.

~ ~ ~

As we stand under the jets of warm water wearing only our underwear, the soothing liquid cascades over us... Theo slowly trails his tongue along the side out my neck. We entwine our fingers. "Eden," he breathes, "you make me feel sensations that I've never felt before. I have this strange feeling of lightness in my head and my knees feel as if they are weakening."

"So do you, my angel," I whisper.

"What is it? Do you know?"

I arch my back and softly encourage his hand to the side of my silk panties. He begins to caress my hip in such a sensual manner that I am now feeling more than lightheaded. I feel as if I am about to lift off...

"Untie my panties for me, baby, and then I will tell you what's causing you to feel like this."

While he starts to plant sweet, little peppery kisses down the centre of my chest, I hook my fingers into the band of his boxers and slowly ease them down over his lean hips. He nuzzles into my chest and I stroke his hair. His soft lips locate my nipple and he starts to flick his tongue over and around my now- erecting bud. I moan out for him and push his silk further down. He aids me by shimmying out of them and looking up at me. The dreamy look that's exuding from this man's eyes is one of a pure, delicate innocence and I am honoured to the woman he chose to be in his presence. While his cock nudges against my belly, I kiss him and whisper, "I can't wait to feel you inside me and by the way the strange sensation that you are feeling I believe is *love*."

He breaks into the most enigmatic smile, and as his fingers make deft work of my underwear, they float to the floor. He sighs, gently turns me around and tenderly begins to lather my hair.

THEO'S THOUGHTS

I've been yearning to feel her skin contacting with mine and now that I have her in my arms, the sensations that are coursing through my veins are ones of pure hedonistic enchantment. I release my hands from her soapy hair, turn her around and gently ease her to the shower wall. While I tentatively dip my tongue in the hollow just below her neck, I arouse and as she tilts her head backwards, she lets out a sexy moan that's tinged with the syllables of my name. I repeat my actions. I hear my name again and I free fall into her soul. I have never felt anything like this in my life before.

The way Theo is washing my hair is so soothing. He's gently massaging the shampoo into my scalp while kissing me on the side of my neck.

"You're beautiful, baby," he murmurs. "You are so sexy and feminine and every inch of you is mine."

He lets go of my hair and turns me around. The water continues raining over our bodies, his tongue finds the sensitive spot that lies below my neck and that is when I feel as if I am floating up in the air. His hardness is now nudging into my belly. I ask him to pour some shower oil into my hand. He does. I slip my hand down over his taut abs and locate the hair that is just below his happy-trail. He hitches a breath and asks for me to caress him. I curl my hand around his erection and start to work his magnificent length.

"Oh, baby," I breathe, "you feel positively divine."

He moans out my name as I slowly continue rolling his cock from root to tip. He buries his head into the side of my neck and gives my flesh a little nip. I sigh with pleasure. He responds to my sound by telling me that he is now going to take me to his bed.

"Good," I respond, "because feeling you throbbing away in my hand, I don't think I can wait another moment to feel you buried inside me."

~ ~ ~

We drop our towels to the floor. He drapes his arms around me and draws me into him. He nudges me a little and I feel the surround of the bed brush against my lower back. Within a moment, the closeness between us is not just one of a physical – it's more of a rare and precious mental connection. As I feel his heart beating in unison with mine our bodies align and our souls whisper soft secrets to each other. Our newfound love is filled to the brim with a yearning, with a red hot passion for more than just lovemaking. It's craving to be nurtured like a freshly planted seed. It requires feeding and watering continually to blossom, so with these thoughts whirling around my mind, I ease myself from his damp, warm embrace, back away from him, sit down on the edge of the bed and shuffle myself upwards until I rest my head upon the array of soft, sumptuous pillows that adorn the head. I extend my arm to him. He crawls onto the bed, places his shaking hand on my palm and points his lashes down. He doesn't say a word. He's gone incredibly shy on me. I wonder why. I draw him into me and as our bodies realign, we both shudder at the warmth of each other's skin. He now appears to be showing signs of nervousness. I can tell by the way his lips are quivering on my neck and his body's slightly trembling. Something's telling me that it might be his first time. I must admit, since we first met, I have had my suspicions that it might be but I couldn't come to a conclusion on that thought.

It couldn't possibly be? Could It?

I stroke his hair to soothe him and find myself asking him the question. My heart melts when I hear him bashfully murmur, "Yes, Eden, This is my first time. I've *never* made love before."

I am the woman who will soon be claiming not only his untouched body but the depths of his beautiful, uncharted soul.

A multitude of confused thoughts run through my mind… Why is a man so alluring, so sexy and so intelligent still a virgin? Is that by choice or fate or both? Is he too shy or is he just a beautiful old-fashioned soul who wanted to wait until he was either deep in love or married? I push them all to the back of my mind. I don't want anything to spoil our moment, so I lighten the mood by asking him how old he is.

He stops shaking and divulges his age. My heart flips when I hear that he is a mere twenty-one.

"I know what you are thinking, Eden," he whispers, "you are thinking not only is he a computer geek, he's also a very strange man not to have had sex before."

"I'm not, baby. No. I would never think that of you."

"Really," he exclaims, "you don't think I'm weird?"

I laugh to break the tension and assure him that I don't. I tell him that I find it flattering that the first time he is going to make love is with me. He looks at me and asks, "How old are you?"

I don't hesitate and I tell him. He sighs and chuckles, "I have a fetish for older women."

We fall into hysterics of laughter and I playfully swat his chest.

"You cheeky devil," I giggle. "I'm only five years older than you."

He arches an eyebrow and groans, "Well, Ms. Mature, are you going to show me how this love-making lark unfolds or am I going to have work it out on my own?"

I wrap my legs around him and angle my hips up towards him. He shudders and tells me that before we make love, he has something he wishes to give me. He fumbles around under the pillow that I am resting my head upon and locates what he is looking for.

"Put your left hand on your chest, baby."

I do. He gently runs his thumb and forefinger along my wedding finger and I miss a breath as I watch him slide a platinum band encrusted with diamonds over my nail and settle it down at the base.

"Will you marry me, Eden?"

My mind is now in a total whirl. I mean, here I am, lying in bed, naked with a twenty-one year old sex-god of a virgin that I've only just met and he's asking me to marry him! This has to be the most bizarre situation I have ever encountered. I can't speak because he's now resting on his haunches and his glorious erection is distracting me from answering.

He frowns at me, grabs the sheet and covers his lower body. He takes a deep breath and continues. "Stop ogling my cock, Eden. I assure you, you can have it after you have answered me!"

Gosh, he's so cheeky!

I sit upright and kneel in front of him. I place my left hand over his heart tattoo. The light catches the diamonds and the glint dazzles my eyes. I look him straight in the eyes. His beautiful violet irises are sparkling brighter that the jewels on the ring, and as I answer him, he closes his eyelids. I wrap my arms around him and hold him tight. We stay like that for an endless moment, just safe in each other's warm comforting embrace. Moments silently pass us by until he draws back a little from me, beams me the most delightful smile and declares, "I want you to know that my ring is a sign of the deepest love, a love that will last for eternity. Every time we have to be apart, you will always have a piece of me with you because our initials are inscribed inside the band."

I'm stunned even further by his words, his gesture and his depth of love for me!

"So, my fiancée," he chirps, "do I now have your permission to kiss my wife-to-be?"

I flop myself back on the bed, sigh and tell him that I would love to receive a kiss from my husband-to-be. He whips the sheet away from his person, gently lays on top me and skims his lips along mine.

"I feel a little anxious, Eden."

"It's going to be all right," I comfort, "I will lead you. I promise you once we connect with each other you will soon find your way."

He slips his hands under my buttocks and I aid him by tenderly curling my fingers around his erection, slowly rolling his thick, firm length.

"Jeez, Eden," he moans, "your hand curled around me... It... It... Please don't stop touching me in this way." He kisses the side of my neck and I continue to stroke his cock until he whispers to me that he thinks he can't take any more of my handiwork and could I please tell him again how he feels.

I circle his crown with the pad of my thumb and as I feel the warmth of his pre-cum seep onto my skin, he asks again, "Baby, how do I feel to you?"

"You feel pretty spectacular throbbing away in my hand, my angel. In fact, I think it's time I felt you inside me."

He rests on his elbows, gains a little confidence from my words and winks at me. The pure untimely sexiness of his batting lash breaks the tension between us and we both let out an ice-breaking laugh.

"You ready, Theo?"

"Eden," he murmurs, "I'm really nervous… what if I don't please you?"

"Hush, baby," I calm, "trust me, you have nothing to fear." I place my palm over his *two* hearts and tell him to follow what lies within his soul, and I assure him that in an instant his body will naturally take the reins.

He takes a deep breath and I spread my legs a little more for him. I close my eyes and he gently lifts me into him. Slipping into me with such ease, I welcome him into my body with a grateful moan. His lips hover above mine. "Kiss me, baby."

He skims his tongue over my lips and tentatively inches into me. I gasp out as his hardness stretches me and my muscles clench him tight. His face is amazed with wonderment. Hitching a breath, he whispers, "Eden, you are beautiful. You feel so divine… I think I could get lost in you."

The look of concentration coupled with the glaze that's now veiling his eyes is so mesmerizing that to see a man in lost in this moment is more than just an honour, it is a privilege. Suddenly he pauses and I ask, "Are you all right, Theo?"

He responds to my sexual tone by softly declaring that I have become his addiction. I half-close my eyes and instantly become lost with each slow, fulfilling stroke that he sets. I sink even further into lust, into love with him as I see the tiny flecks of gold that are prominent against his violet irises, ignite with a deep, burning passion. Each glimmer entices me further in to his fathomless sea of love. I'm drowning in his hypnotic melt and I don't want to be saved. He's kissing me in a way like no other that all I can manage to whisper is, "Everyone has an addiction and you, my darling just happen to be mine."

Increasing his pace, his mouth clamps down upon my flesh. Each tiny draw on my skin increases… He sucks hard and my heart does something mysterious when he tells me that he's leaving a secret love note buried within my skin… the sound of his heaving breathing and the flush that's spreading across his chest heighten me further and I instantly cum. He stills and as the tiny beads of sweat fall from his forehead onto my cheek, he closes his eyes and in a surprised tone, he murmurs, "You came for me? I made you cum?"

THEO'S THOUGHTS

Her angelic breath is now lightly caressing my lips and she's teasing my soul, taunting my heart with her suggestive whispering of enticing words. The yearning to feel her tongue scrolling around mine is almost becoming too much to bear. I close my eyes as I feel her body ripple over my cock in pulsating waves. I hitch a breath as she drenches me in her cum. I am in awe at the sensation that's making it easier for me to grind into her. I keep the rhythm, and as the beads of sweat drip from my forehead and fall upon her cheek I can't help myself from breathing to her that I can't believe she came for me and that I made her cum.

I ask him to open his eyes. He does. I melt as I see the veil of misty lust mirrored between us. I clench him again and he groans…

"Yes I did and yes you did! You see, there's nothing to worry about."

He increases his rhythm and starts to pound hard into me while explaining to me how I feel clenched around his cock. Each explicit detail he breathes, coupled with his lips sucking on my neck, weakens me even further.

"You feel perfect, Theo, just perfect," I encourage. Well, he does. He is.

I'm now so lost within the lust that's shining in his captivating eyes; I feel as if we are thousands of miles up in the air. As he creases his brow and the beads of sweat glistening upon his skin send me weak, through his erotic groans he tells me that he loves me. With each increasing stroke of his hardness filling me, I arch my back, and as he whispers over and over how much he adores me, he worships me; I clasp his buttocks tight and push him as deep as possible into my quaking body. His increasing rhythm is now stirring another orgasm within me. "Tell me you love me. Eden," he pleads, emphasising my name. "I need to hear you tell me."

I kiss him lightly on the lips and offer, "I love you, Theo. I will always love you."

"Good," he groans sexually and then stuns me by asking my permission to allow him to cum.

My plea of a 'yes' is the trigger for him to release. Our bodies shudder around each other's. He fills me with his warm fluid and envelopes me in his arms, kisses the tender spot on the top of my shoulder and runs his nose along my neck. His soft whispering breath that falls against my flesh once again never fails to excite me. He reaches my ear and gently nips my ear lobe. "You smell divine, Eden. So much so, I can't inhale enough of your captivating scent."

I nuzzle into him and breathe in his Theo after-sex fragrance. "So do you, baby."

We stay in bed for what seems like hours, drifting in and out of love-making and light slumbers until neither of us can physically take any more and we curl up in each-other's arms and fall asleep.

~ ~ ~

While I rest here upon Theo's back, I lay replete in the aftermath of our first love-making session of the day. There is something so beautiful, so peaceful listening to his breathing as it slowly returns to its regular steady pace. I run my fingers along the back of his neck and he shifts slightly under the lightness of my touch.

"Well, that was beautiful way of saying good morning baby, I love you," I murmur into his ear.

He rolls over and his lips curl into a smile. "I love you too," he yawns.

I wrap my arms around him and he curls his legs around mine. "Did you feel what I felt when we made love?" I whisper.

He begins to stroke my hair and tells me that he felt something that he never encountered before. I melt when he bats his lashes at me, and in a soft, gentle tone inform me that the next time we are in the throes of making love, he will tell me exactly what he felt.

"Okay, I'll hold you to that."

"Hmm, you know what would be perfect right now?"

"No. Why do you enlighten me?"

He breaks into a boyish grin, slides his hand between my legs and quietly murmurs, "Spending the whole day making slow, sweet passionate love with you… the beautiful future Mrs Caro."

I smile, agree at his suggestion and ask him what his surname means.

He wraps his arms around me, and in a whisper-of-a baby's-breath, he offers, "Beloved."

THE GENTLE DOMINANT

PRELUDE

As his warm lips connect with mine, he softly breathes,

"By the time I have you pleading with me to let you cum, you will have precariously balanced on the precipice of erotica for the first time of many times. You will realise that I have now become the man you want to wake up to every morning, and when that most precious thought infiltrates your mind, it will curl around your heartstrings and pluck at them like a virginal harpist who knows nothing about the instrument that she's nestling between her thighs. You will readjust your thoughts accordingly and align them with mine. It will be then, without any questions needed, that you will find yourself easily adapting to the single most powerful thought of all – and that notion is that I have now become your hardest goodbye."

CHAPTER ONE

I lean over the protective barrier that separates the general public from the trail of actors and actresses weaving their way down the red carpet and stick out my glossy copy of the première programme as far as I possibly can in the hope of capturing the leading man's attention. I, along with the other hysterical fans, wave it around in the air like it is a celebratory jubilee flag. He is now sauntering his way down the pathway and heading in my direction. I'm desperately hoping that he will notice plain little me at random and choose to sign my programme. All I've ever desired, apart from seeing him in the flesh is to also see his signature stained in ink. I stare intently at him, and as he's becoming closer to me, I can now easily study his gorgeous features. Greedily drinking in every square centimetre of his chiselled cheekbones, his ski slope of a nose and the mop of dark silky curls that tumble over his forehead, my tummy flips when he momentarily flicks his tongue over his lower lip. This man is most definitely even more captivating in the flesh than on the silver screen. While he continues ambling his way down the screaming line of puppy-eyed, love-sick women, I shiver as he, signing a teenage girls copy, averts his attention from her, cocks his head to one side, breaks into the most enchanting grin I have ever encountered and winks at me!

Oh help! Darius Carter just batted those enchanting, long dark lashes of his at me!

I bow my head to stop myself from being on the receiving end of another possible lash bat but as I do, the deep, honeyed tone of a sexy voice jolts me back to reality and when I raise my lashes, I *meet* the owner of said voice. That is when I can't halt myself from blushing because the voice belongs to him… the man who is standing on the red carpet… Darius Carter. He is the man I constantly fantasize about; he is the man I have just sat watching on the open-air screen act for the last two and a half hours. Strangely he doesn't sign my paper; instead he carefully extracts it from between my trembling fingers, gives me a rather heart-melting smile and focuses directly upon me. I am drawn to his sculptured lips, and as they move I can't hear what he is saying to me. I transfix upon him for what seems like minutes… The noise of the screaming crowd is phenomenal and it's drowning out each one of his precious words. Handing me back my paper, I take it and as I go to say thank you, he turns and casually continues to move on down the row. I frown and curse under my breath at the women around me. If only they had toned their noise down, I might have actually caught a few of his words. I go to drop the programme to the floor. What's the point of keeping an unsigned one? But as I go to release it from my fingers, something prevents me from doing so. I glance at it and my heart goes into an irregular rhythm when I read the black scribbles strewn across the glossed paper:

DINNER 8.30 SHARP ~ HOTEL FLORENCE ~ PENTHOUSE ~ MY DRIVER WILL ASSIST YOU ON THE BEGINNINGS OF YOUR JOURNEY.

DC

The adrenaline is now pouring into my bloodstream at an uncontrollable rate; my mouth is rapidly dehydrating and my hands are starting to quake. I clumsily stuff the programme into my jacket pocket, and as I feel a light tap upon my shoulder, I gather myself, spin around to see a rather dashing gentleman dressed in a smart, black suit standing in front of me. He gives me what I can only describe as a kindly, fatherly smile. Tipping his peaked forage cap to me, he then – in such a matter-of-fact-tone – clearly states, "Good evening, Ms. My name is Giorgio. I am Mr Carter's driver."

My knees now weakening, I gaze into his eyes, which are exuding a gentle softness and somehow I manage to find my voice. It waivers a little and a 'hello' squeaks from the back of my throat.

Smiling, he continues, "I would like to say that it's a pleasure to meet you, Ms. And since you *are* having dinner with Mr Carter this evening, he wishes me to drive you to his temporary residence here in London, but first, on the way, he suggests we stop off at a boutique of his choosing and purchase you a suitable black, halter-neck dress for this occasion."

Still in shock from reading Darius Carters scribbles, I can't utter a single word in response to Giorgio, so instead, I croon my neck, peer around him and my vision immediately homes in on Mr Carter. He is leaning up against a black, sleek sports car and he has the most alluring and beguiling look upon his face. He gives me a little curt wave and immediately disappears around the other side of the car.

Looking back at the man in front of me, I stutter, "But… But…"

Giorgio offers his hand to me and I place my dampening palm in his. With his other hand, he gives me a light reassuring pat. "Come, Ms," he gently offers, "Mr Carter is so looking forward to meeting you. He asked me to tell you that it will be an honour for him to have dinner with you, and if I may say so, what could possibly be nicer than an evening of light conversation and fine dining with a man of his grace?"

My head now in a total whirl, I can't respond to him, so I give up on questioning the whys and wherefores of this bizarre situation. By squeezing his hand, I agree to accept the invitation and I let him lead me towards the waiting limo. Giorgio opens the car door for me and ushers me in. I seat myself down and as I turn to one side, searching for the clasp to secure my seatbelt, I feel something being placed onto my lap. I fasten myself in, and I look down to see three red roses tied with luxurious green ribbon.

Attached is a small white envelope. My hands now shaking like never before, I extract the card from its host and my heart almost misses a beat when I read the handwritten inscriptions.

Helena, a piece of your heart will always be nesting in mine.

DC

How does he know my name?

CHAPTER TWO

I stare in the ornate full-length mirror and wonder what on earth I am doing here. I feel as if I have been transported into some kind of magical and mystical fairy tale and I have yet to turn the last page and to discover the ending of this make-believe story that I have become involved in. I am instantly snapped from my girlish thoughts as the curtain to the dressing room whooshes back and I stiffen on the spot when I see Mr Carter reflected back at me. He's changed his attire and I must say he looks extremely dashing in a causal outfit that consists of navy blue slacks and a crisp white linen shirt. Focusing upon his chest, I notice that the first four buttons are undone, revealing a rather inviting patch of dark, curly hair.

I'm starting to liquefy inside. Moving my vision to his arms, I see his cuffs have been tightly rolled back and they reveal to me a set of strong muscular, golden tanned forearms. *I wonder what it would be like to be cossetted by those arms while I nuzzle into that taut chest of his.* My body now tremoring, feeling a little queasy, I swallow hard, press my palms flush to the side of the mirror and grasp onto it tight. I remain like this for moments trying to compose myself until I feel his presence settling behind me.

Looming over me, he trails his warm palms down my arms until he reaches my white-knuckled hands. Prising my fingers from the sides of the mirror, he brings my arms back a little, releases from me and as they drop to my sides, he steadies me by snaking one arm around my waist. At his touch, I whimper something incoherent and he murmurs into my ear, "Shhh. Just take a few slow, deep breaths and try to relax. I'm not going to do anything you don't want me to do. Is that clear?"

My mouth has rapidly dehydrated and I can't answer him, so instead I just have to nod. As his other hand comes over my right shoulder and slides down over my upper chest, until it halts when he has located the black, silk ties of the dress that are dangling either side of my partially covered heaving breasts, I shiver. Now pressing into me, I shudder again at feeling a fleet of his manhood nudging into my lower back and I let out a muffled whimper as he pushes into me, grasps both ties in his large fist and firmly yanks them upwards. The soft, sensual fabric presses against my nipples causing them to stiffen. Resting his head upon my shoulder, he darts his vision over my cleavage, and as the hedonistic scent of freshly washed male and pheromones permeate my senses and envelope my being, I feel as if I am either about to do one of two things… *lift off or feint.*

"You're beautiful, my angel," he softly purrs. "The rise and fall of your beautiful breasts are absolutely stunning."

I'm now aching to the heart of my inner core and with the heat of his person infusing my senses, I am fast spiralling into such a confused mix of frustration, anger and excitement. I take a deep breath and its now taking all my willpower not to turn around and slap him for being so forward. Grazing his teeth lightly along the side of my neck, he then excites me even further by stating, "Let me tie these flimsy straps around your slender neck. We need to have a safe, *tight* knot and as you get to know me, over time you will realise that I'm rather fond of various kinds of bindings!"

Why I am doing as he asks, I have no idea. I bow my head a little and a guttural groan escapes from the back of this throat. I wonder why he made that sound at this particular moment in time. My head is now in a spin and I am fast becoming powerless to resist him. Tugging the straps tight, he deftly secures them around my nape, nuzzles his cheek in the crook of my neck, and whispers, "I think you need some shoes to go with that hot dress."

Snapping his fingers, he blurts, "Alana! Bring me shoes for Helena."

How does he know my name?

A petite blonde quickly appears by his side and offers him a pair of black Christian Louboutin heels. Taking them from her, he examines them by fingering the satin ribbon ties whilst mumbling that they are just perfect. He then adds: could she please charge the entire outfit to his account and while she is doing so, because she has been so helpful, he wishes for her to choose an outfit for herself. Grasping me by the hand, he swirls me around, and before I can blink, he catches me in his arms. The surprise of his actions causes me to take a sharp intake of breath. Slowly running his fingers down my bare back, the connection of his skin upon mine leaves me completely breathless.

"You are adorable, Helena," he softly murmurs. "There is something so alluring about you, something so beguiling that you hold my attention like no other woman has ever done before."

Stepping forward, he nudges me a little and my buttocks momentarily sweep against something firm. Falling backwards, I land upon a soft seat. Crouching to my feet, he looks up at me and breaks into a stunning smile. Taking my left foot in his hand, he gently starts to massages my toes and tells me that I have pretty, small feet and that he wouldn't mind sucking each and every one on my toes in succession. I openly allow myself to giggle at the thought of it and ask him if he would like to do that right now. Frowning and tut-tutting me, he slips the shoe onto my foot. I am in awe watching him expertly wind the silk ribbon three times around my ankle and fashion it into a bow at the back. When he repeats this action with my other foot, he does it slower than before and the combination of his light touch and the soft, sensuous fabric that is now gracing my person causes me to feel extremely light-headed. A light air escapes from between my lips; he gazes up at me and shoots me such a sexy wink that the air is now followed by my subconscious whispering his name.

I think he heard it. I hope he has.

He rises, extends his hand to me and declares, "There, Helena. You look just perfect and I am so going to enjoy having dinner with you this evening."

Placing my palm in his, and he, like a pure gentleman, aids me to my feet. Drawing me close into him, he soothes, "We are going to be so good together, my angel. I think you understand what I mean, don't you?"

I can't answer that question at this particular moment in time so I ask him why we are leaving through the rear entrance of the boutique and not the front. He squeezes my hand tight and replies, "Paparazzi, sweetheart. Too many of the damn bastards waiting out the front to catch me with you... And, Helena, will you please stop calling me Mr Carter. My name is Darius. It's very irritating considering I am going to get personal with you this evening."

"Oh!" I exclaim, "And how do you propose to do that?"

"It's quite simple really," he wickedly chuckles. "I am going make you cum without entering your body. By the time I have finished teasing you, taunting you, you will be pleading with me to fuck you."

On hearing his words, I stop dead in my tracks, tear my hand away from his, turn to face him and rasp, "You are an arrogant excuse of a man. How dare you speak to me in this manner? Just who on earth do you think you are?"

As the colour rapidly drains from his face and an apologetic glaze casts over his eyes, he offers me his heartfelt apologies and explains to me that he was only jesting and that he will be more careful with his choice of words in the future. Offering me his hand, I swat it away and furiously demand for him to take me home. Stepping towards me, I take a step back. "Take me home, Darius," I implore. "Just take me home."

He narrows his gaze, and within the split of a second, I find myself enveloped within his cosseting embrace. He's hugging me so tight that there is not an ounce of space separating us. Stroking my hair, he, in such a sad, childlike voice, pleas, "Don't leave me, Helena. I'm so, so sorry for what I said. It's just that you do something to me that no other woman has ever done. You exude some kind of magnetic charm… You unnerve me… You make me want lose all control of self-discipline in matters of the sexual nature… You… You"—he stutters and surprises me by blushing—"arouse me… Yet at the same time, your magnetic aura conjures up a vast imagery of erotic and sinful thoughts that continually permeate my mind. I can never explain these thoughts to you and I just hope that maybe over time, you will allow me to demonstrate them to you."

While his words infiltrate my mind and settle upon my soul, I feel a unique calmness surrounding me, and while we remain in hold like this for some time, I am sure I heard him murmur something about star-crossed lovers. When we finally release from each other, he tilts his head to one side, looks down upon me, tips his finger under my chin, tilts my head upwards and breathes one word...

"Stay."

And that simple four-letter word was enough to change the course of my future forever.

CHAPTER THREE

"How long will it be until we reach your home, Darius?" I enquire.

Glancing at his gold Rolex, he cocks an eyebrow and responds, "I'd say about in about half an hour's time. Why do you ask? Are you getting bored of my company already?"

I giggle and say that yes I am very tired of his company and I then surprise us both by suggesting that we could kill some time by sharing a kiss.

His eyes widen at my idea and he then politely asks if he may come and sit next to me.

I smile and tell him that he can.

Seating himself next to me, he then asks if he may kiss me.

I grin and tell him that he may.

He tenderly cups the sides of my face in his hands. I stare intently into his eyes and a somewhat quizzical look glazes over his face. While his now-timeless scent invades my senses, all I can manage to do is close my eyes and imagine what it is going to be like while he kisses me. Will it be like one of his screen kisses – hot, passionate and lingering, or will it be a real genuine, heart-melting and soul-searching one? His fresh breath tingles upon my lips, and as I inhale another soupçon of his fragrance, he dips his head a little lower. Raising my lashes, I exhale as a rogue lock of a curl momentarily sweeps across my cheek. I'm shaking like a leaf at the anticipation of sharing a kiss with him. His lips are now so close to mine that I can feel his breath warming the thin fleshes that coat mine. His eyes are showing me such a deep intensity of passion and I still wonder if he will be acting out one of his screen kisses on me or if it will be one that comes from directly from the depths of his soul. It is as if he reads my mind when he responds, "This won't be just any kiss, Helena. When our mouths meet, this will be a joining of our souls."

What?

Pinning my body with his so I am now flush to the seat, he stuns me by informing me, "I'm going to enjoy tasting the sweetness of your mouth." A luxurious smile lights up his face and while he steadies my face in his strong hands, his eyelids delicately flutter. Pressing his mouth to mine, on the timely collision of our lips, the sensuous kiss he bestows upon me is so captivating that my heart begins to gather speed… I can hardly contain my thoughts. I want to tell him how I feel.

I'm aching to tell him that I've fallen for him.

He continues dipping, darting his tongue between my lips and scrolling it around my mouth. After some time of losing ourselves in each other's hungry mouths, he abruptly draws away and I become confused as I see him shake his head from side to side.

Shuffling upright, I reach out for him but he's already seated opposite me… glaring!

"You seem disappointed in our kiss, Darius," I offer. "Will you please tell me why?"

He doesn't answer. He just averts his gaze, presses the pad of his digit on the intercom button and gruffly asks Giorgio to make haste to the hotel.

~ ~ ~

Darius crosses his knife and fork, takes a sigh and languishes back in his chair. Pushing his empty plate to one side, he takes a deep breath, slowly raises his lashes at me and in a matter-of-fact tone, states, "Helena, I originally wanted the pleasure of your company for twenty-four hours, starting at midnight tonight. But now, after kissing you, I want more. I'm craving to take your body and soul to new heightened places of sexual sensuality."

Startled, I look up from my plate of seared scallops, dab the corners of my mouth with my napkin and decide to be brave and dive head-first into a series of questions. "Why choose me, Darius? Out of all the women you could have, why did you select me?"

An awfully long pause follows my question, and while the moments slowly tick by, I nervously chew on my bottom lip. I pick up my drink and circle the rim of the glass with my finger. He doesn't take his eyes off me. He creases a concerned frown, rises from his seat, pushes it back with a force and walks around to my side of the table. Taking my flute of champagne from between my fingers, he settles it down onto the table and balances himself on the arm of my chair. Tipping his finger under my chin, he gazes into my eyes and offers, "As you so eloquently put it, I carefully choose you"— he pauses, drums his fingers on his chest— "because I do believe I can train you to become the most loyal and loving submissive that a dominant could ever hope for."

On hearing the word 'dominant', I snatch my glass back, sweep it to my lips and drain the entire contents in one swift gulp.

"Whoa, poppet," he softly scolds. "Please slow down. I don't want you inebriated before we even consider taking the first step on our sexual journey together."

I slam my glass down in anger and he – in response – jumps off his perch! I rise from my seat, strut off in the direction of what I hope to be the exit to the foyer while blurting out, "Is that why you wanted to wine and dine me? So you could use my body for your own selfish, perverse pleasures?"

As he angrily stomps after me, I swear I can feel the floor beneath me vibrating, and within a split of a moment he *is* behind me. He roughly grasps me by my waist, spins me around and when I see the menacing, fiery look in his blue irises, I for one am positive that this man is not acting out a drama… He is a commotion all of his very own! Through the daggers of his piercing stare, I rapidly deduct that what he wants – what he seems to require from me – is a genuine request. I had no idea that he was a secret dominant and after all why on earth should I? Holding me so tight around my middle, he shoves his body into mine. The sensation of his hard, rippling muscles that plank his torso pressing into mine coupled with his whispering of seductive and erotic words into my ear is making it so hard from me to gear away from him. He's explaining to me that he will do anything to make me stay and that would include him paying me for my services. My eyes widen at the latter statement, and I try so hard to break free from his embrace but his fingers are digging into my sides and he is nipping the side of my neck in a gentle but stimulating fashion.

"Please, Darius, let me go. I can't do this with you. I don't want to do any of this with you and I most certainly don't want you touching me any more or a single brass penny of your money."

Something quickly charges and shifts in the air between us. Reeling backwards from me, he hangs his head down, quickly apologises and tells me that he will organise for me to be taken home. On raising his head, I see something hidden behind his eyes that I can't fathom. Could it possibly be shame for the way he's just behaved?

"I'm sorry," he mumbles. "I am really sorry for my rather rash and stupid comments. Would you at least let me show you where you would be staying tonight if you forgave me?"

I sigh. He's relentless in his mission to spend time with me, so I soften a little and come to the conclusion that sneaking a little peek at what he wishes to show me won't do any harm because, after all, I am *not* going to stay – but on the other hand, I am ever so slightly curious to see further into his home… his world.

CHAPTER FOUR

He takes my hand in his and leads me up the spiral staircase. Without uttering a word, he just every now and then gives my palm a gentle reassuring squeeze. When we reach the top, I gasp out loud at the view from the viewing balconette. It's positively breathtaking. I can see the twinkling lights of the city of London down below, and as the heavy rain beats down and lashes upon the glass, the glowing bulbs glisten, reminding me of Christmastime.

"By the sound just you made, Helena, I am assuming that you are impressed with what you can see from here?"

I release my hand from his and turn to face him. "Yes, I do, Darius," I sigh with amazement. "It's is absolutely beautiful."

He places his finger to my lips and muses, "Mmm," he pauses and then continues, "It's beautiful and beguiling, just like you."

"Can I ask you a question, Darius?"

"Sure," he chirps. "Fire away."

"How do you know my name?"

He instantly breaks into a fit of mischievous laughter, and without any hesitation at all, he divulges to me that he has been *stalking* me for the last half a year. He tells me that a while back, he was parked opposite a florist's shop, and when he saw me setting up the outside displays of roses and begonias, he couldn't avert his gaze from me and assures me that he will never be able to stop drinking in my beauty. He chortles away and then asks me if I would like to know more about myself. I giggle and say, "Maybe later," because I am now so enchanted by his persona and I need time to process what he has just divulged to me.

Tentatively leaning in towards me, he skims his lips close to mine. His soft breath brushes lightly against my mouth and my subconscious once again taps away in my mind and she nudges me towards a crucial decision. The words tumble fast from my soul as they spill out of my mouth. I divulge to him that I will spend tonight with him and that I will not only honour him with my body but I will also bequeath to him a fragment of my soul. Hovering his lips above mine, he breathes to me the meekest of a 'thank you' that I have ever heard and next he surprises me by not kissing me; instead he retakes my hand in his and leads me down the hallway. We reach the end and he pushes the door open… Once again I am left breathless by the room that that is lain out before my very eyes.

"Helena, this guest room will be at your disposal." He hesitates and continues: "Forever. When you need to spend time out from me, this is where I wish you come to. Nowhere else in the condo, only here must you stay. I hope you will be comfortable here. I shall now leave you to get acquainted with your surroundings. Take a bath or just relax with some music. I shall return for you in approximately one hour."

He drops my hand from his, turns and gently closes the door behind him. I am now experiencing so many emotions that I head towards the French doors, slide them open and step out onto the guest room balcony. Standing in the rain, I enjoy the sensation as it soaks through my dress, and as it slightly chills my skin I am lost within the whole bizarre situation. I am only brought back to earth when I hear a voice infiltrating the elements.

"Helena!" it angrily snaps. "What on earth do you think you are doing? You'll catch your death and I detest the thought of you becoming ill."

I jump out of my skin at hearing the stern tone in his voice and spin around. For some reason unbeknown to me, the look of pure distaste on his face makes me start to giggle. He places his hands on his hips and glares at me.

"Stop laughing, you silly woman. This isn't funny!"

"Oh yes it is," I laugh. "I mean just who the hell do you think you are telling me what I can and cannot do?"

He stalks towards me and slips his hand around the back of my neck, tilts his head to one side and chills me to my core with his icy stare.

"Well, Little Miss Disobedient," he chastises, "are you going to come in from playing in the rain or am I going to have to drag you inside?"

I surprise myself by grasping his free hand and placing it upon my right breast. "Touch me, Darius."

"Helena, please stop," he groans. "This is *not* how it is supposed to be."

My voice alarmed, I sarcastically question. "Then tell me, Oh Great One, how is it supposed to be?"

Ignoring my question, he starts to fondle my breast through the damp silk. Locating my erect nipple, he pinches it so hard that a wail escapes my lips. I toss my head back in response to his touch. Pressing his body into mine, he mumbles, "Fuck, woman. What the hell are you doing to me?"

I can feel his cock now straining against the fabric of his trousers and by god do I want to release the huge beast from its dark holdings. I brush my hand down over his shirt-covered taut belly with the full intention of going lower and unzipping his trousers. He deftly stops me, swats my hand away and growls, "No, Helena. You must never take the lead unless I ask you to."

I see a flash of red. I've had enough of playing *his* stupid game, so I retort in the only way I know." I want you to fuck me right now, Mr Carter. I want you to fuck me right here in the rain. After all, that is what you want me for, isn't it? You want me to be your fuck-toy for a day, so go ahead and get on with it. Damn well hurry up and fuck me!"

Stooping down over me, he states, "You had better learn to control that foul mouth of yours because if you continue to swear like this young lady, I promise you I will have to wash those nasty swear words away with a bar of carbolic soap!"

I reel back from him and hiss that not only does he sound like a bully, he is also a grade-one asshole and I have decided that I am *not* going to let him fuck me. I continue rasping at him that he should either go and satisfy himself by masturbating or order himself in a whore for the night. Stomping past him, I hear him snort.

Chauvinistic pig!

Raising his voice, he demands, "What did you call me?"

"A chauvinistic pig... because that's exactly what *you* are!"

Reaching the sliding doors, he is upon me in a flash. He grabs me by the waist and spins me around. I lose my footing, and as my balance waivers, my back heads towards the wet floor. Saving me from falling, he catches me in his arms. "Helena, if I fuck you now in the mood I am in, I will break you in two. And I imagine you are so tight from lack of use that I shall have to work you with my fingers first before you could easily accept the first thick inch of my throbbing cock."

Bastard pig!

Do I see red at his words? No. I see a whole rainbow of multi-faceted blood-dripping reds and my hand comes up so fast, it hovers inches from his sculptured cheekbone. He catches me by the wrist and I shudder as he glares, "I don't do violence, Helena. If you want a man that will enjoy that type of behaviour, then I suggest you leave right now!"

I break the tense moment by sarcastically retorting, "Hell, you're even more gorgeous when you are cross, Mr Carter. I am mesmerized by the way your eyes flicker with a sexy, glassy glaze and also you make me want to squeeze my thighs together when you curl lips up at the sides. Both of these attributes make me want not only want to kiss you so fucking hard, they make me crave to straddle you, slide down on that overrated famous dick of yours and fuck your stupid, self-centred, over pompous, fucking brains out!"

Now chewing the corner of his lip, he growls to me that I am fast becoming an irritating bitch followed by loudly retorting, "Watch your mouth! Helena… What's coming out of it is abhorrent to say the least."

I smile sweetly at him and laugh. "Fuck off, you stuck-up arsehole! It's my mouth and I will do what I would like to fall from my lips!"

Releasing my wrist, he shakes his head from side to side and wildly mumbles, "I strongly suggest in future that you choose your words more carefully or I swear to you that if you don't I will drag you to the bathroom and soap out your filthy mouth until the bitterness, the sourness of the lather makes you vomit every word of foul language out of your tormented soul!"

Hell, I've really pissed him off!

Now glaring at me, I stick my tongue out at him. He creases a deep frown and what he offers next kills me stone dead.

"And, I may add, I am not impressed by your sarcasm. I think you should leave. This was a mistake. This… We…"—he stutters and then emphasises—"are *not* going to work. I'll have my driver ready and waiting for you in exactly one hour. Take a shower if you wish to warm up. If not, then so be it."

Roughly brushing past me, he snorts! As I hear the door slam exceptionally hard behind him, I wince at the deafening sound of him cursing my name as it fades into the distance.

~ ~ ~

Standing in the foyer, I wonder what on earth just happened. I mean not just now in the last hour but the whole day. All I want now is to be at home, a nice hot bath, a cup of cocoa and snuggle down under my duvet. I step out in the evening's damp air and I see Giorgio holding the car door open for me. I gesture to him as if to say I'm fine and I'll make my own way home. He doesn't approach me; he just closes the door and walks back into the building. I make my way down the street and head towards the subway. I wrap my coat around me and as the rain drizzles down upon me, I start to sob. All I want now is to get home as quickly as possible and erase the memories of today out of my mind. I reach the stairs, and as I go to take a step downwards, I feel a presence behind me. I freeze only to jump out of my skin when a voice booms, "Helena, what the fuck are you doing? You don't think for one minute I am going to let you walk home in the damp, dark of the night, do you? Anything could happen to you."

Relief floods over me in waves at the sound of his voice.

"Leave me alone, Darius. I can run my own life," I weakly mumble. "I don't care for – or neither wish for – you to be anywhere near me. You're just a rich, stuck-up actor… an excuse for a man who thinks he can toy with women for his own pleasure."

Taking a step towards me, I soften as I see his eyes brimming with a soft, sympathetic look. "Not only are you a stubborn mare but you are also a feisty one, Helena. I like those attributes in you."

I thaw a little more on hearing his words and in a somewhat brave tone, I implore him to tell me *exactly* what he wants from me. He doesn't muse or hesitate over his reply. When I hear it, I have to ask him to repeat himself, and when he does, I wilt. I now find myself enveloped in his arms and I bury my head into his chest. Deeply inhaling the fresh scent of his citrus cologne, I say, "You want me to be… to be… your… girlfriend?"

Pressing his forehead to mine in a low, hushed tone, he whispers, "Yes, I do. Is that all right with you?"

"But… but… What about the dominant-submissive element?" I stammer.

"Another time, perhaps…"

I automatically break into a series of childlike sobs, and between my hiccupping I neither muse nor hesitate. I simply answer him with an honest 'yes'.

"Good," he relaxes. "Now that we have that settled, come back with me and let me run you a bath. Let's get you all warmed up and then I'll challenge you to a game of chess."

Pulling out of his embrace, I exclaim. "What? Why do you wish to play chess? I thought you wanted to make love to me all night."

He laughs and tells that there's plenty of time for him to – as I so eloquently put it – 'make love to me' because he's not going to ever let me leave…

I'm stunned!

~ ~ ~

Darius takes my half-eaten lobster roll from me and places it upon the table next to the chessboard. Next, drawing back a chair, he ushers me to sit. I do. Seating himself opposite me, he transfixes his stare upon me and informs me that before we begin our game of chess, he has something he wishes to explain to me. He then asks me if I am ready to listen to what he has to say. I quite simply nod in agreement.

"Helena..." he pauses... "If you decide to honour me by allowing me to become your dominant, this is how I see my service to you."

Leaning forward, he rests his elbows upon the table, half-smiles at me and then continues. "This is my take on what I see our impending D/s relationship not only to contain, but also what may, over time, blossom from the raw intimacy of this moment."

I gulp!

"I see said relationship as being something far deeper and much more emotionally grounded than simply having kinky sex with you. By the same representation, I cannot say that I would align it to ever being positioned upon the plain of a spiritual experience, although I must admit it is possible there are some deep emotions hidden within that most mystical of levels, and who know, maybe one day they can, possibly, without one knowing, become entwined within the tangled web that we are about to weave.

"On balance, for me, D/s is a plateau for relating deeply with you in a manner in which we both must be comfortable with. We must find it satisfactory in all manner of ways."

My mind is now in a whirl at his words and as I go to ask him what I consider to be a very important question, he raises his hand as if to signal my silence. I quickly snap my mouth shut! I am now in complete awe of his declaration that I decide for the moment not to add to his words, as he changes tack and gaily asks, "Have you ever played chess before?"

I pick a chunk of lobster from the plate, pop it in my mouth and shake my head no. A sexy smirk crosses his bowed lips and as they curl up at the corners, he chuckles, "Oh well, never mind. I'm sure a woman as beautiful and intelligent as you will turn out to be a worthy opponent in a multitude of different arousing areas!"

I swallow my mouthful with a nervous gulp and inform him that I don't really understand what he means. He seats himself, stares at me hard and tells me that by the time dawn breaks tomorrow, I will have full knowledge of exactly what he means. Changing the subject, he states, "You're going be the white marble pieces, because I think the virginal colour suits your somewhat innocent personality."

I burst out laughing and I can't help myself from quipping that the colour black would suit him very well because, to me, he appears to be a very dark and mysterious man! He doesn't take his vision off me... The way he's narrowing his eyes while seductively chewing the corner of his lip is doing more than sending a series of ice-cold chills surging down my spine – it's positively engulfing me with an almost raging, burning desire to swipe the chessboard to one side, crawl onto the table, grab him by the lapels of his shirt, yank him hard in my direction until we are so close that we are at loggerheads! Cocking an eyebrow at me, he smirks and then chirpily enquires, "So, Helena, are you going to make your move yet? I wish you would because by the way you are fingering with that poor little pawn, I think you ought to."

"Why?" I titter.

"Well, my sweetheart, it's because from where I am sitting, he appears to be getting damp between your sweaty thumb and forefinger and I fear if you continue fondling him in that enticing manner, he may soon fall from your slippery grasp!"

I groan at his rather descriptive and suggestive response and he in turn responds by leaning over the table and placing his hand over mine. As he does, the charge of electricity that ignites between us causes me to drop said pawn – and that is when I realised that I didn't stand a chance in either beginning the game, let alone the good fortune of winning!

CHAPTER FIVE

DARIUS' THOUGHTS:

I wish to saturate my one and only submissive in words of poetic rapture. She's so precious. My loins are aching for the moment when she will allow our bodies to move in unison. I want to imprint love notes on her delicate skin with each timely nip of my teeth and I'm craving to write with my tongue upon her trembling flesh. I desire to be allowed to let my soul flow freely from my mind. While my darkest, innermost thoughts seep through my veins, it will trail unbroken messages of passion behind it… Each heartfelt letter will infuse through my wrists and they will collate between my thumb and forefinger.

I desire to trace the curve of her spine with my invisible inscriptions and I wish to leave pearlesque trails of my warm fluid upon her sweat-soaked skin. They will forever be indelible secrets that I have never shared with another. I will leave cryptic messages behind… Little bruises of memos that can never be erased, and when I taste her for the first time it will be like reading an unbroken script. While I am lost in sweet infusions of her mouth, the lines merge until all twenty-six letters converge into one and spell out her name…

…Helena.

~ ~ ~

In the dancing, red shadows of Darius' candlelit playroom, I turn my head and have to catch my breath when I see my erotic reflection for the first time in the mirrored wall. She's not reminiscent of me at all...

His scented, oiled hands are travelling at an incredible speed over my now sweat-soaked body. He's teased me in a vast array of sexual ways, and for the last two hours he's had me begging with him to penetrate my body deep... His fingers have been probing me, searching and stretching me in a multitude of undiscovered and unchartered places. Each one opened like a flower in its first innocent blossom and they welcomed his fervent, frantic intrusions with their fragrant but silent aroma.

I was so lost within those moments that when he whispered to me over and over that I must tell him that I will never leave him, I let my soul run free and told him something that caused him to release his hands from me. His reaction was as if he had just been stung by a swarm of bees.

He firmly ordered me to bury my head in the pillow, so I did. Moments passed me by and I heard the opening of a drawer. Not daring to turn and see what he was doing, I quivered as his hands suddenly touched the back of my head. The world went dark and the hairs on my skin erected as the soft velvet went to work and obscured the light around me.

"How do you feel without your vision, Helena?" he asked.

I told him that I felt a little uneasy but also at the same time I was finding myself somewhat intrigued at having to rely on my other four senses. That was the moment when he exited the room and I was left bathed in an eerie silence.

He didn't return for quite a while and I knew that if I moved, he would instantly know. 'How?' you ask? Well, when I first entered the playroom, I scrutinised it so carefully, and for the briefest of seconds my vision fell upon a video camera suspended in the left corner of the mirrored ceiling.

~ ~ ~

Darius' breath is now so close to the side of my neck that as his scent infuses my senses, he whispers, "Do you like breathing in the fragrance of your own sex, Helena? Do you like the fact that it has been an hour since I last touched you and your exotic flavour is still lingering upon my tongue? You may answer me."

"Yes, I do… it does something to me…"

I don't get a chance to finish my sentence because he's interrupted me by firmly ordering me to place my hands behind my back. He's placing one upturned hand in the other and that is the moment when I hear him murmur, "You are going enjoy this part of the lesson…"

I am now so heightened by the thought us being filmed that I don't realise my wrists are being cuffed until I hear the sound of the click of a lock. He commands me to rise to my knees, raise my buttocks in the air to remain face down on the pillow. While I oblige, I feel him tugging at my hair. "It's all right, Helena, don't worry," he reassures, "I'm just fashioning it into a ponytail for you. We don't want your glorious locks getting in the way of our foreplay, do we?"

Kissing me lightly on the back of my neck, I go to make a satisfactory sound but I'm halted from that pleasure when I feel a sharp sting radiate across my buttock.

As I jolt forward, he starts rubbing my now warming cheek, but I don't feel the comfort of his warm skin upon mine; instead I feel something like soft, leather caressing me.

"We need a safe word for this part of our game. I think in light of our recent chess game, we should use… checkmate."

~ ~ ~

"You like that, don't you, my angel?" he murmurs, "me rubbing you between your dampening thighs?

"Mmm, I do."

"Good… Now you may now count out loud after each smack of the paddle…

…One…Two…Three… *Smack!*

His voice rising, he demands, "Say it, Helena! Say 'one', and after you have, I want you to ask me to continue…"

"*One* – please smack me again, Sir."

"Well done. I am very pleased you called me 'sir', he softly praises, "now let's see if we can make it all the way to the *glorious* number ten."

"*Two*" – oh my! That feels so good and I now have an overwhelming desire to scream for him to fuck me.

"*Three*" – the heat is bearable and pleasurable at the same time.

"*Four*" – the adrenaline is seeping into my venous system at an alarming rate and I am now feeling so turned on.

"*Five*" – his breathing is deepening and he's making a carnal sound. It's a grunt that I've never heard from a man before.

"*Six*" – he's nipping me on my shoulder and praising me for making it over half way.

"*Seven*"– fuck! That was really hard… almost too hard.

"*Eight*" – I don't think I can take much more… '*Checkmate*' fleets through my mind and almost rolls off my moisture starved lips…

"*Nine*" "pl—please… Stop!"

"Safe word, Helena", he demands. "Say it and I promise you I will stop!"

I hold back my *word* of safety and he growls, "No? Then I shall continue… just one more strike and then we have baseline of ten improve on in the future."

"*Ten*" – my thighs are now aching and every nerve ending that I possess is positively burning, screaming out for him to probe me with his fingers and let me cum. On the tenth contact of the paddle, as the red-hot pain sears through my stinging, dry skin, I try so hard to stop myself from showing him that I can't take any more and as the wetness that's pooling between my thighs threatens to release of its own accord, I manage a whimper of desperate plea for him to let me cum. He doesn't chastise me for asking. That really does surprise me.

I hear him drop the paddle to the marbled floor and a sense of relief fills me. On hearing the unzipping of his jeans and I shift slightly as he leans over me and whispers that because I have been such a patient and quick learner it is now time for my reward. He informs that I must *not* cum until he has. The next sounds I hear are the groans and grunts of a man in the rapid throes of hand-fucking his cock, and the next sensation I feel upon my body completely takes my breath away. A warm fluid splatters onto my buttocks and the primeval, carnal moan that escapes from deep within his throat is positively enthralling. I cry out for him and as a few drops of my own warm, pent-up liquid starts to release and drip down my inner thighs, he roughly parts my legs and gives an unsatisfactory grunt. He tells me that I still have a lot of patience to learn to control but considering that this is my first lesson, he will choose to ignore my disobedience.

He removes my blindfold, and as he gasps a fistful of my hair, he orders me to turn and look at him. I do. The serious look upon his face excites me even further. He cups my centre in his palm, briefly massages my swollen nub and slowly slips two fingers so deep into me that they press upon my now full bladder. Working me to and fro, he commands me to cum for him. As sweet release floods from my aching body, he sucks hard on the flesh of my neck, and while he does, he tells me that he is leaving secret love notes within the deepest layers of my skin. His words alone spiral me into the most earth-shattering orgasm I ever experienced in my life. He stops probing me and chillingly breathes, "You are perfect, sweetheart. You are just pure, innocent perfection and I am going to enjoy tainting you."

I lay panting while he releases my wrists from their hold. He then lifts me into his arms and I am carried out of the room while he informs me that he is now going to bathe me.

CHAPTER SIX

As he lowers me into the warm scented water, the first slight of the liquid against my buttocks causes me to let out a little yelp. Lifting me out, he hovers me over the bath, and in a concerned tone asks, "Is that too hot for you, Helena?"

"No, it's fine," I reply. "It's just stinging a little on my bottom."

"I'm sorry it smarts," he sheepishly replies. "I'll soothe it for you later with some of my 'magic' body crème."

I'm puzzled at what he means, but nevertheless I manage a nervous laugh. He fully immerses my body into the tub, and as I become accommodated with the tingles of light pain that are radiating across my cheeks, he tells me that next time he spanks me, he'll go a little easier on me. While the light scented water swathes my aching body, he says, "Stay forever with me, Helena. I have so more to teach you and surely you can see how compatible we are becoming."

He begins to massage my shoulders, and even though the water is warm, I shiver beneath the bubbles.

"Will you stay?"

I tilt my head backwards and close my eyes. "Of course I'll stay," I murmur, "after all I am your girlfriend now, aren't I?"

He releases his hands from me and I hear him walk around the bath. "Open your eyes, sweetheart."

I do and what I see of him next, sends my head into a giddy spin.

This is the first time I've see him naked.

From the top of his head to his toes this man is pure perfection. His dark, curly hair is a mop of an unruly mess and as my vision travels over his taut torso, I see a pinking scar just left of his tummy button. *I'll ask about that later.* I follow the line of soft dark hair that cascades down his chest until I halt at his groin. I openly and unashamedly lick my lips when I see his rather impressive manhood stiffening.

Grasping his thick, veined cock in his hand, he gives it a slow, teasing, temptous roll and chortles,

"Is my dick impressive enough for you, Helena?"

"I don't know," I jest, "I have yet to see how it performs when it's inside me!"

He cracks a filthy grin and asks me if I would mind him joining me in the bath. I giggle and reply that considering it's a rather vast hot tub, he may. He steps in and bears down upon me. His deep-blue irises are alight with a burning passion for me and for me alone. He stares at me without blinking and in a soft, whisper of a breath, my name leaves his moist, glistening lips…

With the full weight of his body, he's pinning me down to the tub and the way he's started teasing me, taunting me with his hardness is driving me to point of a wild, crazed insanity.

"For heaven's sake, baby," I breathe, "would you please just stop tempting me and hurry up because I am desperate to feel you inside me!"

Raising an eyebrow to me, he says, "You called me baby… That's quite forward, you know!"

I giggle again. Prising my legs apart with his knee, he muses, "Mmm … How frantic are you for me?"

"So much so that I don't think I can take any more of your games," I quip.

He grins and tells me he has more games up his sleeve and if I play this one to his satisfaction, he will introduce me to some new ones, adding that there is one particular game that he particularly likes and that merriment involves the use of a riding crop! He then lets out the most unbelievable sexy chuckle, one that causes shivers to run through my hips and collate at my now-aching centre. Licking his lips, he informs me that because I took my spanking well, he is going to get me so frustrated that I will be writhing underneath him – and not only will he have me begging for mercy but he will also have me *climbing the walls*.

I burst out laughing and quiz, "How on earth do you propose to get me climbing the walls?"

He rests one arm upon the rim of the tub and the other on my shoulder. "Like this," he growls. He retreats slightly, whispers my name, circles his crown against my folds, thrusts deep into me and hisses, "Just like this, baby. I'm going to grind into you five times and five times only and then I'm going to lift you out of the bath, take you to my bedroom, strap you down to the bed and devour every inch of your body with all manner of exciting play toys and we shall begin with this…"

I do more than more than draw in my breath when I see the 'toy' covered in bubbles that he had just extracted from beneath the soapy water… I almost faint! *Almost.*

BREAKFAST

On reaching the bottom step, I smile as I see Darius casually lounging up against the kitchen work surface sipping on his morning coffee. His taut, naked torso is still damp with beads of moisture from his recent shower, and his hair is a ruffled, damp, unruly mess of glorious, thick curls.

Taking another sip of the aromatic dark liquid, he places his cup down onto the surface. Hooking his thumbs into the top of his sweatpants, he yanks them down a little…

"You like what you see, Helena?" he teases.

I laugh and tell him that yes, I like very much what I can see, but how on earth am I going to concentrate on eating my breakfast while trying to abstain from desiring him – could he at least please put on a tee-shirt? He chortles away and pushes his sweats just that little bit further down so I can see the soft, downy hair that lies beneath his belly button. Moistening his lower lip, he cocks his head to one side and in a sexy drawling tone, chuckles, "After last night's playtime, are you now hungry for something other than my famous salmon bagels topped with crème fraiche, my angel?"

I rub my smarting wrists and giggle. "I could be."

"Mmm," he mutters, "I'll think about feeding you with my body in a little while, but for now, this man's tummy's doing a mega rumble, so come, my angel, come and sit with me and let's eat."

Nearly fainting at him calling me his angel, he approaches me and pulls me into his arms. "You're not going to pass out on me, are you, Helena?"

"Well, if you feed me some of that wonderful creation that's sitting on the table over there, then I think I might start to feel better."

He presses his body into me. "Come on, let's eat because I too need some energy. In fact, I need barrels of the stuff because, my precious, after we've eaten, I want to fuck you again until we are both a dripping wet heap of a sweaty mess of hot, scented sex."

Oh!

He then changes approach and melts my inner core, asking, "Stay with me Helena. I need you." There is not a damn thing I can do to stop the emotions that are stockpiling in my soul. "You make me have a dull ache in my chest... I have never felt that before."

His love flows over me in a crashing, forceful wave...

Wrapping his arms around me, he inhales the scent of my hair and again pleas, "Please don't leave me, Helena. I...I..."

When I see the soulful glaze in his stunning blue eyes, I hush him with the most gentle of kisses while murmuring to him that I know what he is trying to say…

…*And I love him too.*

"FORTHY-EIGHT HOURS"

"FOREVER YOURS"

TAKEN FROM "STOLEN MOMENTS"

QUANTUM ENTAGLEMENT

Two atoms may collide and separate, never to meet again.
Others can stick together by virtue of the chemical bonds they form, until the day that bond is broken.
But there is another type of connection that is far more powerful and 'romantic'.
Certain objects can become linked by a mysterious process called entanglement.
Particles that become entangled are deeply connected regardless of the distance between them.
If they become separated by the width of the universe, the bond between them remains intact.
These particles are so deeply linked that it's as if they share the same existence.

...And tonight, as the sound of the metronomic roar of the oceans waves tease the bleached, white sandy shores of the Indian Ocean, in the soft, flickering glow of the scented candles that are casting their dancing shadows upon our damp, naked skin, we will find ourselves allowing us to take that leap of faith...

...We have been longing to do that for so, so long. As our bodies align for the very first time, the sensuous, light touches of our trembling skin melding into one rapidly turn into the first of a series of delicate but hungering kisses. That meeting of our mouths slowly evolved into a novel of silent, passionate secrets. We are eating each other slowly with unbroken words of love and we are relishing in devouring each other's lost souls with an abundance of passionate heartfelt kisses.

As the moments of undying love pass us by and the brave new dawn peeks at us from the horizon, we find ourselves being utterly and totally captivated by each other's mystical and magical silent thoughts.

~ ~ ~

DAY ONE

I lean over my gorgeous, sexy man and whisper, "Hello, baby, I love you so much."

He beams me the most enchanting smile, and as he does, my heart flips because, you see, we have both been yearning for this most precious of moments to occur for a vast expanse of time.

He blinks, and while I watch his chest rise and fall, he – in almost a whisper of a baby's breath – breathes, "Hi, there gorgeous… And I love you too. I always have."

I fall a little closer to him, and while his fingers chart the topography of my spine, I shiver with delight. I deeply inhale the captivating scent of his cologne, and as the base notes of white musk and cedar invade and enrapture my now heightening senses, I find myself instantly lost within an ever-expanding dimension. He bats his divine lashes at me, and as I see the love exuding from his crystal-azure eyes, I liquefy inside because this is first time we that have ever been this physically close to each other. I can hardly believe this is happening to me – to us –and when he tenderly snakes his hand around the back of my head, he draws me a little closer to him and breathes, "Do you know what you do me, beautiful?"

I am now lost within this most sensuous of moments and as I go to answer him, his arms curl around my naked body, and in a split second I find myself pinned beneath him. He's now bearing down upon me and the sexy, mischievous grin that's lighting up his face is a true picture to behold.

"When I kiss you, sweetheart," he softly whispers, "it won't just be a meeting of our lips, it will be the joining of two souls that have been aching for so long to feel the moment when each other's hearts finally entwine."

Oh, what is this man doing to me? I can barely take any more of his endearing words, and while his hardness nudges against my belly, my mind screams to tell him how much I love him… my subconscious is positively wailing at me, urging me to express the abundance of undying love I have always felt for him.

"I feel a little anxious, baby," I declare. "Do you know what effect you have on me?"

"Yes, I do," he smiles, "I always have… but you have something so captivating about you that I can't bear the thought of never being without you."

He shifts above me and I spread my legs a little wider for him. I close my eyes, and as his hands slip underneath my buttocks, he gently lifts me down until I feel his crown nudging at my centre. While his lips hover above mine, he murmurs for me to kiss him. He skims his warm, moist tongue over my lips and our mouths finally, gently meet. He tentatively inches his hardness into me and I groan out as his thick, manhood stretches me. My muscles instinctively spasm around him. His eyes, oh my goodness… his eyes are alight with the dewiest glaze I have ever seen in a man, and as he starts to set the rhythm, something begins to well up inside me and my body lets out a little contractual shiver.

Hitching a breath, he buries his head into the crook of my neck and softly declares, "You are so beautiful. Your body feels so compatible joined with mine… It's as if our bodies were specially crafted for each other."

The look of concentration coupled with the heavenly, dreamy look that is now veiling his eyes is so mesmerising that to see a man captured within this moment is more than just an honour, it is a privilege. I tilt my head backwards and stretch my neck in anticipation for another longing skim of his soft plump lips. While his wet, warm hand travels over my sweat-sheened breast, he lightly circles the sensitive skin surrounding my already erecting nipple. In response to his feather-like touch, I can't help but moan out his name. He's now weakening me further, and when he grasps my bud between his thumb and forefinger, he applies a little pressure to it and coaxes it into a hardness that I have never encountered before. As the dampness now collates at my aching centre, he settles his other hand between my thighs. I shiver as he circles my nub, and while he tenderly works me into a heightened frenzy, the corners of his lips curl up.

Grinning away at me, he continues exciting me and I can't help but beg, "Baby, please let me cum. I don't think I can take any more of your sensual teasing."

He lets out a deep, throaty chuckle, pushes his hardness deeper into me and in such a sexy tone, he breathes, "Tell me how much you are craving for me, my sweetheart. I want to hear you plead for me."

The combination of his rather delicious taunt and his enchanting voice are making me feel light-headed. I am now encountering a strange new sensation. It is as if I am lifting off and there is no way I can come back to Earth until I have experienced my first orgasm with him. We are now eye-to-eye and I am totally in awe of the pure, dreamy glaze that veils over his stunning blue eyes. Now feeling totally and utterly ready to give myself to him, he honours me with the ultimate of hedonistic displays – what I can only describe as a well retained *pièce de résistance*:

That was the moment when his mouth met the sensitive flesh that coats the side of my neck, and as his lips drew onto me, he told me that was leaving indelible love notes upon my person. Each one he graced me with was going to be a series of secret coded messages that only he and I would ever be able to decipher. I was so lost within the aura of my man that I let my inhibitions go. My body shuddered… His rapidly followed and as we both came in a joyous unison, we simultaneously admitted to each other that we have always loved each other.

*I always have loved him without knowing when or why...
and one thing I do now know for sure is
that we will always be a part of each other.*

*For we are and always will be
two rogue particles that have now become entangled, and we
are deeply connected regardless of the distance that was once so
expansive between us.
Even though the width of the universe separated us for a while,
the bond between us has always remained intact.
We are so deeply linked that it's as if we have somehow always
shared the same existence.
We are one.
We have become a whole.
We are us.*

~S~

Made in the USA
Lexington, KY
27 January 2016